In the dystopian world of 2653, Arnia Powell, a police officer in Vancouver, discovers a shocking truth about her past.

Arnia receives a letter written by her deceased mother that reveals that she was not her mother's biological child, but a foundling discovered as a newborn in a hollow tree in Oregon's Valley of the Giants, wearing only a mysterious golden pendant around her neck.

When she is assigned a new partner, Shepherd Daniels, she is surprised to find that he shares a remarkably similar story. Shep was also found as a newborn in a hollow tree in the same forest, wearing an identical pendant.

Human. Alien. Hybrid. Arnia and Shep's journey to uncover their past leads them on a collision course with destiny, where the future of two worlds rests on their shoulders.

This book is a work of fiction. Names, characters, places, and incidents either are products of the author's imagination or are used fictitiously. Any resemblance to actual events, locales, or persons, living or dead, is entirely coincidental.

ARNIA'S SHEPHERD
Copyright © 2025 Gabriella Bradley
ISBN: 978-1-4874-4313-9
Cover art by Martine Jardin

Published by Extasy Books Inc

Look for us online at:
www.extasybooks.com

ARNIA'S SHEPHERD

BY

GABRIELLA BRADLEY

CHAPTER ONE

"Officer Powell. In my office! Now!"

Arnia was just about to head out of the station to go home after a grueling evening shift when the captain's commanding roar echoed through the precinct's hallway. She froze in her tracks, and her stomach lurched. Now what? The captain liked to pick on her, sometimes for the smallest things. She couldn't think of anything that had happened that day that he could fault her for. The only reason she had come up with for why he always picked on her was that he was racist. She was the only African American woman in the precinct. At least partially... She thought she was African American. She really had no clue. Her skin was quite dark, but unlike other African Americans she'd met, her hair was straight, not true black, and she had dark blue eyes. She hurried to his office and ran into Scott Turner, her partner, on the way. "I got called on the carpet. No need to wait for me, Scott."

"You sure? It's cold out there, and it's late."

"It's fine. I'm dressed for it. I'll walk home. See you in the morning." She continued to the captain's office. His door stood ajar, and she hesitantly entered.

"Yes, Captain?"

"How often do I need to tell you not to let juveniles get away with theft? Today is yet another example."

A name flashed through her mind. *Little Johnny...* She'd

1

caught him stealing a loaf of bread that day. "Captain, the child was—"

"Hardly a child, Officer!"

"He's only ten, Captain."

"A small-time miscreant already! You tend to forget that the troop of young hooligans he's a member of will soon be in their teens. Our streets are overrun by teenage gangs dealing in crimes far more severe than stealing bread. Remember, Officer Powell, even a minor crack can bring down a mighty dam. You've been a police officer for four years and should know better. I think you're too soft for the job. Perhaps you'd be better off sitting behind a desk."

A pang of fear shot through her. He wouldn't… Would he? Inwardly, Arnia cursed Scott, who had undoubtedly reported her to the captain. The thought of being deskbound scared the shit out of her. "I'm sorry, sir. It won't happen again."

But it would…except she was going to be a lot more careful from now on and watch Scott like a hawk.

"This is your last warning."

"Understood, Captain."

"Before you leave, this was delivered for you today." He held out a large manila envelope to her. "Dismissed," he barked as she took it from his fingers.

She barely glanced at the envelope and left his office. Last warning? She'd only been caught twice being lenient with a youngster, and both times by Scott. It was on the tip of her tongue to again speak in Johnny's defense, but she thought better of it. The boy had stolen the bread, but it was for his ailing mother and two very small siblings. They lived in one of the alleys, their home a few ragged blankets held together by pegs and rope. Arnia had stealthily followed Johnny one day to find out what he did with his stolen booty and, at times, had covertly left some of her own rations outside the tent.

She took off her bulletproof vest, uniform jacket, weapons, and belt, shrugged into her worn leather jacket, stuffed the envelope into a pocket, and took her backpack out of her locker.

An icy wind and snow greeted her when she stepped out of the precinct. More for the homeless to deal with… How many of them would become ill or succumb to the sudden temperature drop?

She walked the long trek home deep in thought, arriving at her apartment building without realizing it. David Taylor, the guard on duty that night, opened the door for her.

"Cold out, Arnia?"

"I'll say."

"They're predicting at least twelve inches tonight."

"Oh, joy! See you later." She hurried up the stairs to the fourth floor and quickly headed for the communal bathroom to have a quick wash at one of the basins and brush her teeth before going to her room.

A minute past midnight curfew, the lights flickered off, and the building became quiet. After peeling off her uniform, she quickly crawled into her bed. If one could call it a bed. It was a very hard, thin mattress on a wooden platform. But she was one of the lucky ones who had been able to get a furnished room in the large building that had once been a luxurious hotel. Furnished? It had a bed, a narrow closet, one chair, an old mirror, and a little rickety table.

Her room was hardly bigger than a closet. When they converted the hotel into a habitat for the homeless, each room was stripped of all amenities. The hotel had been divided into more than two thousand rooms, some a little bigger than others, for those who had children or were a couple. If you were lucky enough to get a room and could afford to pay for it, it beat sleeping on the streets or in stairwells, especially during the cold winter months.

Each floor had a large communal bathing facility open from 6 a.m. until midnight. The bathroom had a row of ten toilet stalls, ten washing basins, and ten showers that were on timers. Adult residents were allotted a ten-minute shower once a week, and children were given five minutes. Because of the cameras, there was no cheating, no trying to slip in for an extra shower. People who had tried this in the past were evicted. She hated the cameras, but they had to be there in case of trouble between males and females. When she had her weekly shower on Saturdays at 6 a.m., she tried to position herself so that not too much was visible to whoever was monitoring the screens or any men who were using the other remaining showers.

Arnia had been able to buy a small flashlight on the black market, enabling her to read after the lights were turned off at midnight. She shivered. Along with the lights, the heat was also turned down to a minimum, and it was December. With this cold front, the temperature in the building was going to plummet fast. She pulled the ragged blanket up and leaned on her elbow, her flashlight aimed at her antique book.

Books were a rare luxury. She'd read the two she had so many times that she could almost recite them by heart — *Gone with the Wind* and *The Lord of the Rings*. Both books had cost her most of her savings, but they had the power to imagine herself as a heroine and be part of an imaginary world.

She was fortunate to have an education, thanks to her mother, who worked as a maid for an elite family who insisted Arnia join their children during tutoring time. Her education resulted in her being accepted into the police academy when she turned eighteen. She sighed and swallowed hard, still feeling the pain of losing her mother, who had succumbed to tuberculosis at a much too young age just a few months ago. Her mother had lost her job and ended up on the streets. By the time Arnia found out, she'd barely had enough time to search for her and say goodbye. Tuberculosis was rampant among the homeless, but when the two children of her mother's employer got their BCG vaccine, Arnia was lucky to have received it with them.

She couldn't get into the book tonight, so she closed it, put it under the mattress, sat on her knees, and opened the blind that covered the small window. Vancouver lay swathed in a virginal blanket of snow. A less picturesque scene unfolded below of homeless citizens huddled together against the biting chill of winter. Shadowy figures, desperate for relief, fought over the brief flashes of warmth birthed from burning oil barrels. The sight of small children exposed to such harsh conditions struck a painful chord in her heart, knowing that many would not live past this brutal season…

The city was a mess…

The world was broken…

Would it ever stop and go back to what it once was? Not that she'd ever experienced any of what it used to be like, except seeing it in pictures, but her mother had told her tales of before extreme poverty struck and when there was enough room for everyone… When the air was so much cleaner to breathe…and more importantly, when almost no one went hungry. Her mother had heard those tales from her grandparents, stories that were passed down through the generations.

But all that was centuries ago. Everything went to hell after the alien invasion in the year 2089, and now it was 2653. Earth had never recovered from the worldwide overnight stealth attack by hundreds of alien ships that had destroyed and bombed so many towns and cities. The aliens had plundered and killed millions and left a devastated world behind when they left.

Suddenly, she remembered the mysterious envelope in the pocket of her jacket. She got out of bed and retrieved it. While carefully opening the envelope, she went back to bed. Who was it from? Did it have to do with work? Pulling the blanket around her, she placed the flashlight so that she could see.

Now really curious and also a little afraid of what she would find inside, she pulled out a folded sheet of paper and a smaller envelope. The paper was a single sheet. After unfolding it, she smoothed it and held it near the flashlight. It was signed by Evelyn J. Rivera, her mother's former employer.

*

Dear Arnia,

I hope this letter finds you well. I am so sorry for the delay in getting it to you. We only recently found the envelope taped at the back of the chest of drawers in your mother's former room.

All the best,

Evelyn J. Rivera.

Short and sweet. Except Evelyn Rivera had *not* been that sweet. After all, as soon as Arnia's mother became sick, Evelyn had tossed her out on the street, fearing she'd catch the dreaded disease. Lung tuberculosis was extremely contagious.

Arnia angrily crumpled the paper into a ball, tossed it to the floor, and then looked at the smaller envelope. Her throat became constricted when she saw her name written on it in her mother's familiar handwriting, and she carefully tore it open. It felt thick at the bottom. She opened it wider and held it upside down. Something dropped out of it. She picked up the flashlight, shone it on whatever it was, and gasped. The object lay sparkling in the light—a golden chain with an intricate pendant. If it were real gold, it would be worth a fortune on the black market, but there was no way her mother could afford something so valuable. It was probably paste, a piece of fake jewelry discarded by Evelyn. It didn't matter. It was something left to her by her mom, a small token to remember her by.

She fingered the chain briefly, then picked it up and slipped it over her head. The pendant nestled between her breasts. For some reason, it felt warm and comforting. She stroked the pendant for a moment, fighting threatening tears before concentrating on the other envelope, but yanked her hand back when a strange, tingling feeling shot up her fingers and into her arm. "Static from the cold," she murmured.

This envelope contained two sheets of paper. She took them out with trembling fingers and unfolded them to gaze at her mother's handwriting.

For a few moments, her eyes flooded, and she swiped at the tears, then swallowed hard before focusing on the letter.

My sweet girl,

Now that I know that I'm very sick and am going to die within a month or two, it is time I reveal the secret that I should have told you a long time ago. And I even debated on telling you now, as I don't know if it will do you any good, but it weighs on my conscience, and I feel deep down that you need to know the truth.

Arnia let the sheet of paper drop to the mattress and wiped her eyes again. *The truth? About what?* Her mother was one of the most honest, sweet, loving... What could she be talking about? Her father? The elusive figure who had always been an omnipresent phantom in their lives. She had never known her father, and since her mother had told her nothing about him, Arnia thought of him as merely a sperm donor. Maybe the letter would finally reveal the truth about him, about her roots…

You are not my biological child. Yet, despite that, you have always been my daughter, and I couldn't have loved you more if I had given birth to you myself.

The revelation tore through Arnia like a gale, leaving her dazed and motionless, leaning back against the cold wall. Her racial identity had always been a source of intrigue, considering her mother's pale features, blue eyes, and blonde hair, which contrasted sharply with her own dark complexion, much darker eyes, and almost black hair. But she'd attributed it to probably having an African American father. She'd never asked her mother because she had always been so reluctant to answer questions about him. And now she knew why… After she'd digested this information, she picked up the letter and continued to read.

As you know, I was born in California and orphaned when I was twelve. From what my mother told me, I had no other family. Like so many, I was suddenly homeless, scrounged and stole, and somehow survived. I heard tales and rumors that things were better up north in Canada. So, when I was nineteen, I decided to go to Vancouver. As you can imagine, it was no easy task on foot, and it took me a long time to get there. When hiking through Oregon, I was attacked by a couple of hooligans who stole a bunch of my things. An old man had seen it, and he advised me to avoid the main roads and hike through the forests. He told me that it would be safer for me. So I did. Honey, describing the giant trees I saw is almost impossible. I wished so much for a camera. Some of the trees had trunks bigger than a house. Thankfully, there were hollow trees

8

where I spent the nights, or sheltered from the rain

One evening, I carefully checked out a hollow tree in which to spend the night to make sure there were no animals inside, when I heard the cry of a baby. I looked inside, and I found you. You were newly born, maybe even that day, because the wet cord still dangled from your belly, and you were naked and still covered in cheesy patches. There wasn't even a towel, a cloth, or anything. The only thing you had was the chain and pendant around your neck, which I'll enclose in the envelope. I checked it out. It's real gold... And no matter how poor we were, I kept it for you all these years. I wrapped you in my blanket and looked around for a few hours for a woman because, surely, whoever had given birth to you still had to be close by. But after wandering around the forest for a while, I found no one. I didn't know what to do, but it was getting late. I stayed in another hollow tree.

Several days passed, and no one showed up looking for a baby. I had nothing with which to cleanse you except leaves and my hands. Nothing to feed you. And all I had to keep you warm was my old, ragged blanket. In desperation, I let you suckle. Even though I had no milk, it kept you quiet.

After several days and nights, I gave up and continued to hike. During this time, I fed you drops of water. It was all I had, and you surprised me by surviving. I carried you next to my skin, wrapped the blanket around both of us, your little head near my breasts, and hoped to come across a town soon. I didn't.

After leaving the forest, I stumbled upon a hut belonging to a very old woman. I believe she might have been indigenous. She was very old and lined and had long white braids. She asked why my baby cried so much, and I told her I had no milk. She gave me some soup and told me to wait while she searched for some herbs. When she returned, she set about cooking something, and when she was done, she told me to drink it and said it would help me produce milk. I stayed with the woman for a few weeks. She was kind, taught me how to care for you, and even gave me scraps of material to use as diapers. And to my surprise, I began lactating. When I told the old *woman – I've forgotten her difficult name – that I was leaving and going on to Vancouver, she said I was better off living in the wild, like her. And maybe she was right. But I could not see myself hunting for animals or skinning them, and I had no knowledge of herbs.*

The woman offered to teach me, but I couldn't see myself keeping you. She stocked me with dried meat and herbs that sustained me during the long journey to Canada. I managed to get across the border and eventually arrived in Vancouver. Which, much to my disappointment, was no better than LA or San Francisco.

Weeks passed. You were thriving, and though I planned to take you to social services or maybe a hospital, I couldn't do it. You had crept into my heart. Being able to breastfeed you bonded us even more, and it was as if you were my very own baby. And the gods smiled upon us because soon after arriving in Vancouver, I got the job working for the Riveras, and I was able to give you a half-decent upbringing and a roof over our heads.

Now you know the truth. And more than likely, you will never know who you truly are, where you came from, or who your true parents are. You were mine...body and soul. Your past didn't matter to me, but now that you know, you may want to investigate your origins. As a policewoman, you might be able to find out some things. I love you, baby girl, more than life itself. Please don't hate me for what I did. Forgive me for keeping this secret.

Your loving mother.

Arnia let the letter slowly sink to the bed. Hate her? If her mother hadn't kept her, she more than probably would have died inside that tree. If her mother had taken her to social services or the hospital, where would she have ended up? With whom? And maybe no one would have wanted her, and she'd have ended up in one of the overflowing orphanages...

Do I really want to discover who I am and my roots? What kind of woman could have abandoned a newborn baby? Nope, Mom. I'm not going to dig into that mystery even if it were possible to find out how I ended up inside that tree, which it is not. You were my mother and always will be, and I'll be forever grateful that you rescued me and took care of me...

CHAPTER TWO

Arnia put on her uniform and boots, looked in the old mirror, slipped into her jacket, and headed out the door to work.

When she got to the lobby and saw the snow, she sighed. Plowing through more than a foot was going to be a chore. Getting to the precinct would take her at least an hour and a half, if not more. She debated calling Scott to pick her up in the patrol car. They were supposed to take turns driving it home, but she always let him take it because he had a family to get home to. Most of the time, he gave her a ride home, but she usually walked to work in the mornings.

She began the long trek. At least it had stopped snowing, and the wind had died down for now. The odd vehicle whizzed past her. Several of them still had regular tires, splattering her with snow and mud. Not that many people had aircars. They were a luxury that only the very wealthy could afford.

While she walked, her mind dwelt on the letter and what she had learned about herself. Countless possibilities flitted through her mind about the woman who had given birth to her and abandoned her. Maybe she had gone to look for help and got lost. Maybe she had died… It really didn't matter now. However, in a way, it did matter because now Arnia was curious about the circumstances of her birth, her roots, and her history. But even though she worked on the force, tracking down who had left her in that tree was impossible. Unless the woman was listed among the thousands of missing persons and children... But even then, without any more details, it was a chance in a million that she'd discover anything. She shrugged it off. It didn't matter...

Her comm pinged. "Yes, Scott?"

"Where are you?"

"On my way to work."

"Walking? Why didn't you call me and wait for me to pick you up? I've told you so often that I can give you a ride in the mornings. After all, you always let me take the cruiser."

"And I've answered you just as often that the exercise is good for me, and I don't want to bother you."

"Don't be ridiculous. I'm almost at your building now. Just wait for me, okay? I'll be there shortly."

But she continued to walk, though at a slower pace. Standing still in the below-zero temperatures, she'd freeze her butt off. It didn't take overly long for Scott to pull up beside her. She quickly got into the patrol car.

"Hey," he greeted.

"Hey, yourself."

"What's new?"

Her hand went to the pendant hidden by her jacket and uniform. So much was *new*... She was sorely tempted to tell Scott everything. But though they'd been partners for four years, they weren't really close. Not close enough to share personal stuff. He would probably tell the captain...just like he told the captain almost everything she did. And this was private...precious...

"Nothing new," she lied. And for him, it wasn't. It really was none of his business.

Once at the precinct, they clocked in. Arnia put on her duty belt, made sure all the weapons were secure, removed her jacket, put on her bulletproof vest, and then put on her uniform jacket. She was ready. Scott was still dawdling when the captain's voice sounded over the intercom.

"Officers Powell and Turner, to my office."

"What the hell does he want?" Scott muttered while quickly putting on his duty belt, vest, and jacket.

"Who knows. Hurry up, or he'll have a fit."

When they walked into Schmidt's office, he growled, "Took you two long enough."

His next words shocked her...

"Officer Powell, meet your new partner." He gestured at an officer leaning against the wall. "Until he gets to know Vancouver, you'll be taking over driving the patrol car."

Really? Just like that, with no warning? So like him to pull such a stunt... Arnia hadn't noticed the man leaning against the far wall when they had entered. Glimpsing at him briefly, she nodded and introduced herself, "Arnia Powell."

Why was Schmidt breaking up her and Scott? He had been her partner ever since she graduated from the academy. Now she had to get to know and get used to a stranger.

"Turner, you've been reassigned to the Abbotsford division."

"What? I never put in for a transfer!" Scott almost shouted. He grunted. "Captain, that's more than an hour away, and I don't have a vehicle. How—"

"I guess you'll have to move," the captain responded. "You've got a week off to make arrangements, starting today."

"That's fucking impossible. I've got a family, and—"

"Nothing is impossible. You can always bunk at the precinct and go home when you're off."

Arnia felt Scott's pain. Why hadn't the captain sent her? She had no family... "Sir, I can go in Scott's place," she offered.

"They don't want a woman. Sorry. Dismissed."

"Scott, I'm so sorry," Arnia told him while leaving the captain's office.

"Hey, you tried. Thanks for that."

"By the way, since no one bothered to introduce me, I'm Shepherd Daniels. Shep, for short," came from behind them.

Arnia stopped and turned around, almost bumping into her new partner. "Sorry. I already told you who I am."

"Yes, my new partner, Arnia Powell. By the way, I'm from the Langley division." He added with a disarming smile, "Never thought I'd get hooked up with such a pretty cop!"

She had to look up. He was very tall. Electric blue eyes gazed into hers. He had blond hair, a clean-shaven, angular face with a deep dimple in his chin, and lips made for kissing. This new partner of hers was to die for… "Do you have a family, Officer Daniels?"

"Please…call me Shep. Nope. No family. Well, a mother and two sisters…but no wife or kids. You?"

"Eh, no." She turned and looked at Scott. "I guess this is goodbye. Good luck in trying to relocate your family in such a short time." She felt so sorry for him. It was difficult enough to find accommodations at the best of times, let alone if one had a family… Scott had three young children.

"I might have to do what Schmidt suggested for a while. Sally is going to be so pissed."

"Do you own your place?" Shep asked.

"Hell no. Who can afford to buy a house or apartment on a cop's salary? You found a place to stay? The place I've got is designated as a family unit. Otherwise, you could have taken it."

Shep shrugged. "Well, you could have inherited a house from your parents, right? No, I haven't looked for a place yet. I wasn't aware I'd be expected to start today. Thought I'd have enough time, at least a week, like you. What's accommodation like around here?"

"Eh… Have you seen the streets? This is Vancouver, buddy," Scott said sarcastically.

"Isn't it the same everywhere? I thought finding a room in the big city would be easier."

"You could try the building I live in," Arnia suggested. "It's not much, just an old, converted hotel. It's cheap. Turnover is quite rapid. We need to get going. I'll drive you by during patrol."

"I guess I'd best take off and tell my wife the great news," Scott said in a sarcastic tone. He grasped Arnia's hand and squeezed it. "I wish you all the best, Arnia."

"Thanks. You, too, Scott. Good luck with the move. If you hang around for a few minutes, we'll give you a ride home." She didn't think the captain would mind. It wasn't that much out of the way of the patrol route anyway…

CHAPTER THREE

After dropping Scott off, Arnia drove back to the patrol route.

"I felt his pain. Kind of unfair to do that to a cop who has a family. How long have you been partners with him?" Shep asked.

"Just over four years."

"Wow. That's quite a while. I guess you'll miss him. Not to worry. I'm easy to get along with."

But it did worry her. Would Shep report her to the captain if he caught her helping those in need? *I'm going to have to be extra careful until I figure him out...*

A report came through about a shooting in progress. Arnia could never understand how people still managed to get their hands on weapons, especially the old-fashioned kind that still fired lethal bullets. Though...phasers were just as lethal. Just not as messy... The black market, yes...but so many of the culprits had no job, no income. They survived by stealing, preying on the innocent...

"First day on the job and a shooting?" Shep said in clipped tones.

"Get used to it," Arnia told him. "This is East Vancouver. Are you wearing a vest?"

"No, I—"

The radio crackled to life, cutting him off.

"All units, more shots fired at East Hastings and Gore.

Possible multiple victims. The suspects were last seen fleeing east on foot. Any available units, respond immediately."

Arnia's grip tightened on the wheel. "That's us," she said, flicking on the siren. She quickly glanced at Shep. His chiseled jaw was tense, and his attention was locked on the road ahead.

"Let's move," Shep said, bracing himself as she gunned the engine.

They wove through traffic, lights flashing and siren blaring. Arnia had handled high-pressure calls before, but this one felt different, not because of the situation but because of who was sitting beside her. Shep was new, untested, and — as much as she hated to admit it — distractingly handsome. It was one thing to learn to work with a new partner… It was another when that partner had a face that belonged on a billboard or magazine cover.

"Ever been first on the scene for a shooting?" she asked, taking a hard left.

"Not lately," he said, voice steady. "Did two years in Toronto and four in Langley before I got transferred to Vancouver."

She raised a brow. "You've seen some action."

He smirked. "You could say that. You?"

"Too many to count."

Dispatch cut in again. "Shots still being reported. Bystanders on scene. Proceed with caution."

Arnia reached for the radio. "Copy that, dispatch. ETA two minutes."

They turned onto Hastings, and the scene hit them like a punch to the gut. People were screaming and ducking behind parked cars. A man lay sprawled on the pavement, blood pooling around him. Another clutched his arm, groaning. A woman in a torn jacket pointed frantically east.

"They went that way!" she shrieked. "Two guys, dark

hoodies. One had a gun!"

Before she could tell Shep to stay put because of the lack of a vest, he was already out of the car, hand on his holster.

Arnia ran to the injured man on the ground. He was barely conscious. "Sir, can you hear me?"

The man coughed, his breath ragged, blood trickling from his lips. "They shot… Didn't even see 'em coming…"

Blood soaked his shirt. Arnia pressed her hand to the wound. "Stay with me. Ambulance is on the way."

Shep was at her side in seconds. "He's in bad shape. Other guy's stable, arm wound." His eyes flicked to the darkened alley where the suspects had fled. "We need to move before they get too far."

Arnia scanned the street. More sirens echoed in the distance — backup wouldn't be long. But every second counted.

"You up for a chase, rookie?" she challenged, testing him.

Shep grinned, hand on his weapon. "Rookie? Born ready."

She took the wounded man's hand and placed it over the wound. "Keep your hand here and press hard as you can," she told him, then turned to Shep. "Stay behind me. You're not wearing a vest."

They sprinted toward the alley, but Shep didn't stay behind her. He was right by her side. The air was thick with tension, and Arnia felt the adrenaline surge through her veins.

As they reached the alley's entrance, the glow of a flickering streetlight barely illuminated the narrow passageway. Garbage bags were piled high against a chain-link fence, and the unmistakable clang of a metal dumpster shifting echoed ahead.

"There," Shep whispered, pointing toward movement near the far end of the alley. Two figures wearing dark hoodies were slipping around a corner.

"Police! Stop!" Arnia shouted, drawing her phaser.

The suspects bolted.

Shep didn't hesitate. He took off after them as fast as he could on the slippery surface, his long strides eating up the distance. Arnia was right behind him. Her breath came fast as they dodged snow drifts and debris. *Wow… He can run!*

One of the suspects turned and fired. The shot cracked through the quiet alley, ricocheting off a dumpster. Arnia ducked, heart pounding. "Shots fired! Shots fired!" she barked into her radio.

Shep veered left, using the alley's shadows for cover. "I'm flanking!" he called out.

The second suspect hesitated for a split second—enough time for Arnia to close the distance. She lunged, tackling him hard against the alley wall. He grunted in surprise as she twisted his arm behind his back, forcing him down. "Stay down! Hands behind your head!"

While she cuffed the perp, she threw a quick glance at Shep. He was still in pursuit of the other gunman, but Shep was faster. He lunged, grabbing the guy's hoodie and yanking him backward. The gun clattered to the ground. The suspect fought back, throwing a wild punch that caught Shep across the jaw. Shep stumbled but recovered fast, ramming the suspect against the wall. "That's all you got?" he growled, pinning him with force before snapping cuffs onto his wrists.

Arnia finished cuffing her suspect and called it in. "Two in custody. Send EMS and more units to secure the scene."

She met Shep's gaze across the alley. His chest rose and fell with exertion, but a triumphant glint shone in his gaze.

"Not bad, rookie," she said, smirking.

He let out a breathless chuckle. "Not bad yourself."

She stepped closer, just close enough to see the faint bruise forming on his jaw. "That's gonna hurt tomorrow."

Shep tilted his head, smirking. "You volunteering to ice it

for me?"

Arnia rolled her eyes but couldn't help the small grin that played at her lips. "You wish."

Shep leaned in slightly, lowering his voice. "Guess I'll just have to take more hits if it gets me your attention."

A flash of sirens bathed them in red and blue as backup arrived, breaking the moment. Arnia shook her head, but the electric moment between them lingered.

Shep gave her one last sidelong glance as the suspects were loaded into the back of squad cars. "Hell of a first chase together. You surprised me."

"Surprised?"

"Yeah, you're just a little thing. The way you tackled that guy… Very impressive."

"You didn't do half bad yourself. But dammit, Shep, you're not wearing a vest. That's asking for it."

"There were two thugs. You couldn't handle both of them. That's why you have a partner. I'll wear a vest tomorrow. I promise."

"We've got the night shift tomorrow. You hungry? I wouldn't mind some lunch before we head to the station to type up reports."

"I also need to look for a room, somewhere to live, or I'll end up bunking at the station for the night."

"We can drive by my building after work."

CHAPTER FOUR

Arnia held her watch over the scanner. "I'm paying for both," she told the cashier. "My welcome treat," she told Shep over her shoulder.

He'd grabbed one of the fake burgers. How he could eat the cardboard imitation beef was beyond her. Although many ate it...she couldn't. Having grown up in a rich household where she enjoyed real food with the Rivera children, she could never get used to the faux meat. It wasn't that noticeable in chili or spaghetti, but burgers? Her lunch consisted of a small salad, fries, and a coffee.

They ate in silence. Shep finished quite fast and grabbed a couple of fries off her plate. She smacked his hand. "If you want fries, go buy some," she snapped.

He undid the zipper of his jacket. "Warm in here."

Suddenly, she noticed the chain around his neck and the pendant dangling from it. It was identical to hers... The chain was heavier, but there was no mistaking the pendant. "Where did you get that?"

"Get what?"

"The pendant on your chain."

He was quiet and gazed out the window at the snow coming down. "It's snowing heavy."

"Yes, it is. That doesn't answer my question."

"Eh...it's kind of personal."

"Then I guess mine is personal, too," she spat at him and

pulled the chain from beneath her shirt and vest. "Identical."

He shrugged. "It's fake, and there are hundreds of them around."

"Where did you get it?" she pressed.

"I've had it for a long time."

"Bullshit. It's as real as mine. Fake jewelry loses its luster after wearing it often, and the gold will peel off."

"Leave it alone, Powell."

Why was he so mysterious about a stupid chain and pendant? Especially after she'd shown him hers. She tucked the chain and pendant back. Once again, while touching it, she'd felt the strange vibrations. The chain was static. Maybe from the freezing weather...

After lunch, they hurried to the station to type up their shooting incident reports. She was almost done when the captain suddenly stood behind her.

"Well, Powell, how is the new partner working out?"

She glanced at him over her shoulder. "Fine so far. Hard to say. I've only spent part of a day with him."

"I want you to keep a close eye on him."

"Why?"

"What's with the questions? Just do as ordered. Watch him carefully."

"Yes, sir."

Could this day get any weirder? Why did she have to watch Shep closely? She didn't dare ask more questions, and the captain left.

It was mid-afternoon when they resumed patrolling the East End. "Shep, why did you transfer? Did you put in a request to transfer to Vancouver?"

"Nope. It's probably because I didn't get along with the captain of the Langley precinct. I don't really care. Originally, when I wanted to leave Toronto, I applied to the Vancouver precinct, but the only available opening was in the Langley precinct."

"Why did you want to leave Toronto?"

"My family lives here in Vancouver."

"Oh, I see. And you can't live with them?"

"My sisters are married and live in small quarters, each with a few kids. I can't live with my mother."

"You're so damn mysterious. How did you end up in Toronto?"

"Hey, what's with the interrogation?"

"I'm just trying to get to know you, Shep. We're going to be working together for quite a while. That's if you don't decide to request another transfer."

"I told you. I didn't *request* this transfer. It was dumped on me, and I signed up for two years. You're stuck with me. That's if *you* don't decide to put in for a transfer."

"I'm quite happy where I am."

Nothing else exciting happened that afternoon. Now that she had control of the patrol vehicle, she could take it home. "I'll show you where I live," she told Shep while removing her weapons, vest, belt, and police jacket. "But I can't drive you anywhere else. The captain closely monitors how many kilometers the patrol cars drive."

"And there are rooms available where you live?"

"I can't be sure of that, but there usually are. Be prepared, though. It's a dump."

"Isn't everything if you can't afford a lot?"

"Yup. But you have to put up with communal bathrooms. One on every floor. And you're allowed only one shower a week. But you can use the washing basins any time. Electricity is included in your rent."

"Pretty much the same all over from what I've heard. I lucked out in Langley."

She drove into the hotel's underground car park. Parking was free, and since most of the people living there were poor, virtually no one owned a vehicle. There were tons of parking spaces available. She chose one close to the elevator. "It's nice to have control of the cruiser," she muttered.

"Scott usually had it?"

"Yes. He drove all the time."

Arnia stopped the elevator on the main floor. David stood by the doors, as always. "David, where is the super? I don't see him in his office."

"Oh, sick today. Can I help you?"

"Don't know. My friend here is looking for a room."

"I can assist with that. Two singles are available. One on the sixth floor and one on the fourth."

"How much?" Shep asked.

"Nine hundred and fifty a month. That includes a weekly shower and — "

"He knows already, David. I told him," Arnia interrupted impatiently. All she wanted was to get to her room and relax. That day's events had left her physically and mentally exhausted.

"Sheer robbery," Shep murmured. "And you call that cheap?"

"Look, they just came available, and they'll be gone in no time. Look elsewhere if you like, though I doubt you can find anything that's cheaper. I can't leave my post right now," David said. "If I give you the keys, Arnia, can you show him?"

"Sure." She waited for David to fetch the keys from the super's office. "Follow me," she told Shep after David handed her the keys.

She had no clue why she needed to show him both rooms. The singles were all the same. But in this case, the bed on the sixth floor was broken and the room had no window. The one on the fourth floor was identical to her own and not that far from hers.

"Is there nothing cheaper available anywhere? Closer to

the precinct?" Shep asked.

"Yeah, a tent in an alley... I'll show you the communal bathroom."

"How many rooms here? People?" he asked.

She shrugged. "It has sixty floors, more than two thousand rooms, two elevators, and a mostly empty parking lot. Not sure how many people there are. A lot. Some rooms are bigger for a couple or a family. And it's one of the cheapest places to live."

"I guess it'll have to do. Not that my room in Langley was much better than this. A bit bigger, probably safer, and somewhat cheaper. Where is your room?"

"A few doors down from this one."

"That'll be convenient. I noticed the building is quite a long way from the precinct. But since you've got the patrol car now... I also noticed no hot plate or anything to keep food in. No fridge."

"You've got to be kidding."

"Well, the room in Langley at least had a hot plate and a small mini fridge."

"If you want something like that in Vancouver, you'll pay twice as much, and it would still be a dump. I bought a small microwave on the black market, but I usually buy takeout."

"I guess you could hang a bag out the window during winter to keep food fresh."

Arnia snorted. "They've all been welded shut. Many of the rooms don't even have a window."

"AC in the summer?"

"Are you dreaming? You're forgetting that electricity is rationed like everything else. The lights get turned off at midnight, and the heat is turned down at night in winter."

"The rules weren't quite as strict where I rented in Langley. Then again, that was a room in a large house. Private landlord."

"You were lucky."

"I guess this will have to do. Is there a damage deposit?"

"Yes, first and last month."

"I suppose we have to see the doorman to finalize it?"

"Since the super is away, yes. Let's go downstairs."

After he had signed the contract and paid, he suggested, "How about I take you out for a bite to eat?"

Arnia hesitated. But she had to admit that she was happy he'd taken the room… And now he wanted to take her out for a bite to eat? Did he feel the connection, too? The chemistry that bloomed between them? "Eh, yes. Thanks. But we'll have to walk. Like I told you, I can't use the car during our off time."

He held the door open for her. "And I heard you mention that we've got the night shift tomorrow. I haven't looked at the roster yet."

"Yup. We work from six p.m. to six a.m."

"You'll have to take the lead. I don't know this area at all."

His deep voice sent shivers down her spine. Never before had a man had such an effect on her. *Don't go there, Arnia. It's never a good plan to get too close to a partner…*

She stopped in front of the small diner that wasn't too far from the hotel. "It's small, but their food is good," she told him.

"Not quite what I had in mind, but if you say that the food is good, oh well…"

"What did you have in mind?"

"When I take a lady out for dinner, it's usually to a bit more elegant restaurant."

"This is hardly a date, Shep. And to make it easier, I'll pay for my own food. I quite often buy my dinner here if I feel like something more than a hot dog."

"My, the lady has a tongue…"

"We're work partners," she snapped, opening the door and

going inside without waiting for him.

"Evening, Arnia! The usual?" the man behind the counter greeted.

"Yes, thanks."

"Take out?"

"No, we're eating here." She noticed the man's eyebrows shoot up. She never ate her meals there.

"So, what's good?" Shep asked.

"It's all great."

Shep ordered a burger and fries. As he held out his wrist to pay, she quickly said, "I'll pay for my own."

"Don't be ridiculous."

Arnia opened her mouth to argue, but then clamped her lips together. Instead, she turned and quickly grabbed an empty booth. After Shep paid for the order, he slid into the booth opposite her.

"I don't understand your attitude," he told her.

"Attitude?"

"Yes. Didn't Scott ever treat you to lunch or something?"

"No. He's got a wife and kids. A cop's salary doesn't go far, especially if you have a family to feed."

"Look, I'm not in the habit of taking partners out for lunch or dinner either, but you've been very helpful today, and you paid for lunch. It's my way of saying thank you."

Shifting uncomfortably on the bench, she nodded. "Thanks. While we wait for our food, could you tell me more about the pendant you wear? And this time, don't be so evasive."

"What's with your interest in my pendant?"

"Because it's the same as mine. Identical. I've never seen any others like it. Anywhere. I took a picture of it, researched it online at work, and came up blank."

"How long have you had yours?"

"Just a couple of days. My mother left it to me. It's all I have of her now, it…and her letter."

"I'm sorry."

"For what? Mom leaving me the pendant?"

"You said you've only had it for a bit. Meaning your mother passed away not long ago?"

"She died a few months ago. The letter she left for me didn't surface until just very recently. The pendant was in the envelope."

"Where did your mother get it? Did she always have it?"

"Now you're interrogating *me*. I asked you about yours, and you haven't answered my questions."

Their food was ready. She stood up to fetch it from the counter and set his burger in front of him. "This is real meat."

"Really? Wow. And you eat here often?"

"Sometimes the burger, but they're costly. Most of the time, I just get fries or a hot dog."

They ate in silence, and after they finished, they walked back to the hotel without talking. Arnia stomped to get the snow off her boots. Just before they entered, she asked, "Where is your stuff?"

"At the station. I'll take it tomorrow night. How do I know when I can shower?"

"The rules are posted inside on your door. I shower on Saturdays at six a.m. In other words, tomorrow morning it's my turn."

On the fourth floor, he briefly took her hand. Darts shot up her arm at the contact.

"Goodnight, Arnia. Thanks again for all your help."

"Night," she said curtly, yanked her hand from his, and headed for her room.

CHAPTER FIVE

It was still early, just after eight p.m. Arnia couldn't get into her book. It didn't matter. She'd already read it so many times. Shep haunted her thoughts. And what the captain had said to her. *Keep a close eye on him...* Why? So far, she hadn't noticed anything different about him from other officers—except that he was tall, built, and too handsome for his own good, and he could run faster than she'd ever seen anyone run.

And mysterious...

The pendant...

Why was he so reluctant to talk about it?

She clasped her own and felt the strange vibrations again. It was almost as if the pendant gave off some kind of energy. Yes, he was damn closemouthed about the pendant, almost guarded... Then again, there was no way she would tell him how her mother got hers...that Arnia was a foundling from a tree in a forest and had it around her neck when found.

I need to leave it alone...

It's sheer coincidence that he's got one just like mine...

And how do I know if there aren't more of them around? That was a white lie... And it has to be fake. My real mother is more than probably dead, or was too poor to keep me. How could she have something that was pure gold? Whoever Mom took it to probably lied to her that it was real. It's quite pretty. Why did my birth mother leave me inside a tree? To die? Maybe I didn't cry after I was born. Perhaps she thought I was dead?

Pushing the thoughts from her mind, she conjured Shep's face up in her mind. Instantly, her body was on fire. She squirmed under the blanket as she fantasized his hand between her legs, his fingers playing with the little nub that throbbed like mad...

Blessed relief...

But still his face and smile haunted her, making it difficult to douse the fire he'd ignited within her. Annoyed with herself, she tossed and turned. Some of the officers at the precinct had hit on her over the last four years, but she made it a point of not dating any of them, even if she liked them. Most of them were married or in a relationship now. And she really saw no future for this broken world, no room for a family. Why people still had children was beyond her.

People couldn't afford to pay for birth control...

Earth was beyond repair...

And not just in the USA...

Death, devastation, and poverty were worldwide...

His face surfaced again, pushing morbid thoughts aside, and her body was on fire again...

I have to fight this intense attraction to a man I barely know...

*

The gentle vibrations of her watch startled her awake — it was just before 6 a.m. on Saturday, and she'd slept through the alarm. The vibrations were just a reminder. Arnia groaned softly, blinking against the dim light filtering through the narrow window. Her night had been restless, and she wished she could stay in bed a bit longer, but if she wanted to take her shower, she needed to hurry.

A shiver ran through her as she threw back the thin blanket and swung her feet onto the cold floor. The heating hadn't kicked in yet. Wrapping her arms around herself, she rushed to the small closet, retrieving her worn housecoat. She slipped it on with a sigh, the faded fabric barely offering warmth, then grabbed her toiletry bag, put on her sandals, locked the door behind her, and shuffled toward the communal bathroom.

The moment she stepped inside, thick steam engulfed her, clinging to her skin like a second layer. Voices murmured, water splattered against the tiled floor, and the air smelled of soap, shampoo, and damp towels. Most of the showers were already occupied—naked bodies moved in and out of the mist, some speaking in hushed tones, others washing in silence. She kept her gaze low, avoiding eye contact as she moved to an empty space.

Quickly, she dropped her housecoat on the hook, reached into her bag for soap and shampoo, and grabbed her towel. The water was lukewarm as it cascaded over her body, but she had learned to wash fast. There was no room for indulgence, no time to let the warmth sink into her muscles. Efficiency was key.

She lathered soap over her skin and squeezed a generous dollop of shampoo into her palm, vigorously scrubbing her scalp. The scent of citrus and lavender filled the air, momentarily drowning out the damp, musty smell of the shared space. She had just begun to rinse the suds from her hair when a voice spoke too close.

"I haven't got my stuff yet. Can I borrow your soap and shampoo?"

Arnia's heart lurched. Her fingers clenched around the bottle as heat rose to her face, her stomach twisting into knots. She knew that voice.

Shep.

Her eyelids stayed sealed shut, and she held the bottle out behind her as she stammered, "Y-y-yes. Just grab it."

She had trained herself to be quick, had forced her body into a routine where every motion was precise and swift. Yet, her lengthy hair always took the longest. Ten minutes were up before she even realized it...

A sharp ping echoed through the bathroom, and the water shut off automatically. Her eyelids flew open, and she gazed straight into Shep's blue irises.

Her breath hitched. Of all people... Why? What cruel twist of fate had given him almost the same time slot as her?

His piercing blue eyes flickered, raking over her from head to toe, pausing at her face before flicking back again.

"Are you going to dawdle there, or can I get in before my time's up?" a woman's irritated voice cut through the haze.

Arnia jolted, cheeks burning. "Sorry." She scrambled toward the benches where she'd left her things, grabbing her towel and drying herself as quickly as possible. The thin fabric barely absorbed the water clinging to her skin, but she wasn't about to linger. She wrapped herself in her housecoat just as Shep's timer went off.

Unabashed, he stepped out of the stall, droplets rolling down the sculpted ridges of his chest and arms. The way he moved — confidently, effortlessly, almost gracefully — sent a fresh wave of heat through her.

"Thanks for that," he said, walking toward her. "Again... I owe you." He held out her soap and shampoo. "The towel?"

She hesitated. "It's pretty wet."

"Doesn't matter."

Swallowing hard, she handed it to him. His fingers brushed hers as he took it, the contact sending a ripple of electricity up her spine.

Desperately, she tried not to look at him. She really, really tried.

But her eyes betrayed her.

God, he wasn't just handsome — he was built. Every inch of him was toned and defined as if he spent every waking hour in a gym. And then...her gaze drifted lower.

Her heart nearly leapt out of her chest.

Oh…

Her breath caught at the sight of the undeniable, unmistakable erection facing her.

A mixture of embarrassment and something far more dangerous coiled deep in her stomach.

Shep, seemingly completely unbothered, gave her a lopsided grin. "Sorry for having to borrow your stuff," he said, his voice smooth, almost amused. "But since we can only shower once a week…"

"It's okay," she croaked, her throat suddenly dry.

Without another word, she turned on her heel and all but fled from the bathroom, pulse hammering in her ears. *I forgot to take my shampoo and soap from him…*

One thing was certain…

Saturday mornings had just gotten a whole lot more complicated.

He caught up to her just as she was about to enter her room. "You forgot your towel and these."

"I could have gotten them later. The towel needs to be washed now anyway." He looked adorable with a lock of wet blond hair tumbling over his forehead, the rest of it curling and framing his face. He obviously had no brush or comb either…

"That crossed my mind, too. Are there laundry facilities in this building?"

"No. I take my washing to the laundromat, which is not far from here. You can pay them to do it, or you can do it yourself."

"Good to know. Maybe you can show me where it is later."

"I will. But for now, I'm going to get some more sleep. I advise you to do the same. We've got a week of twelve-hour night shifts starting tonight, and believe me, the nights can be pretty hectic. After dark is when all the hoodlums come out to play."

"We clock in at six, right? I'll meet you at the car, when?"

"About four-thirty. No, wait. It snowed heavily all night. Be there at four."

"But they plow the roads?"

"Only the main roads."

"How long a walk is it to the precinct?"

"Quite a way, and in this weather…would take you more than an hour and a half. I guess you'd like to pick up your things, huh?"

He nodded. "Yes, clean underwear and shaving gear would be nice… Kind of essential. I guess I could wait until tonight."

"Sorry, I can't help you with any of that."

"Hey, I'm grateful that we've got almost the same timeslot. I was prepared just to rinse off. Seeing you in there was a bonus…in more ways than one."

Blood rushed to her face. The innuendo was loud and clear.

"I'll see you tonight." Wondering vaguely if she should ask the super for a different time slot, she took her shampoo, soap, and towel from him and quickly slipped into her room. She leaned against the door for moments, her heart thumping in her ears.

Maybe it would be better to ask Schmidt if she could have a different partner. How would the captain react to such a request? He'd want to know why… What excuse could she give him? Shep made her feel uncomfortable. No, the captain had already asked her to keep an eye on him, for whatever reason. *I really don't want to get Shep in trouble already. He hasn't done anything… At least…nothing that warrants reporting him to Schmidt…*

Warring with her thoughts and cursing softly at herself, she threw off the robe and burrowed beneath the skimpy blanket.

She needed to sleep.

Needed distance.

But when she finally drifted off, her dreams betrayed her.

Because they weren't of cold, snowy streets or looming responsibilities.

They were of him.

Of piercing blue eyes.

Of fingertips brushing against hers.

And of the unspoken, undeniable chemistry that burned between them.

CHAPTER SIX

The shrill beeping of her watch alarm startled her awake. She'd set it for 3.30 p.m., just in case, but she usually only slept for a few hours. This time, she'd slept nearly the whole day. Her limbs felt heavy, her body sluggish, and her stomach growled in protest as she blinked at the dim light filtering through the dirty window. She hadn't even had coffee that morning. Her whole routine was out of whack.

All thanks to the handsome stud a few doors down the hall…

Normally, on Saturday mornings, she would shower, wait a little while for her hair to dry, and then go to the diner for a bite to eat and have her morning coffee before going back to her room to sleep for a few hours. Today, her routine had shifted. The heat from her body still lingered on the mattress, and she could almost swear that the memory of Shep's dream presence clung to her skin… The way he looked at her, the deep timbre of his voice… Slipping her robe on, she grabbed her toiletry bag and hurried to the bath facility to relieve herself and brush her teeth.

As usual, the steam was so thick that one could barely breathe. The fans could hardly keep up with so many people showering throughout the day. While waiting for an empty toilet stall, she quickly washed her face and armpits, chasing away the last remnants of sleep, and then brushed her teeth.

While hurrying back to her room and putting on a clean

uniform, she hoped Shep would be on time so they could stop for a coffee and a doughnut. She tucked her dirty uniform into her backpack, and after hiding her books under the mattress, she slung the backpack over her shoulder, locked the door, and hurried down to the parking garage.

He was already there, waiting. "Morning," he greeted.

"Eh…afternoon."

"Well, since we're doing the night shift, morning for us," he quipped. He rubbed the stubble on his chin. "I guess I'll have time to shave at the precinct?"

"Probably. Depends on the roads." His jacket was open, and she noticed the pendant. "Better hide your pendant and chain. We're not supposed to wear any kind of jewelry when on duty. You should know that."

Now that she thought about it, he had also worn it in the shower. Maybe, like herself, he never took it off?

He tucked it into the collar of his uniform. "Yes, I do know. I forgot to tuck it away. I never take it off."

"I'm surprised it has stayed in such good condition," she said while getting into the vehicle.

"It's solid gold."

"How do you know?"

"I took it to a jeweler and had it evaluated."

"I see. Well, you'd better never leave it out of your sight. The rooms get broken into. Mine has been broken into several times. Guess being a cop makes people think I have weapons lying around."

"Did they steal anything?"

"No. Just made a mess. I've got nothing worth stealing. Two books. But they're classics. Most wouldn't be interested in reading them, and whoever broke into my room probably didn't realize their value. It's a nuisance because it takes the super forever to get the locksmith in to fix the lock. It's a pity we're not allowed to add an extra lock."

"Have you asked?"

She nodded. "Yes, after the first break-in. But the answer was a firm no. All I got was a warning to hide anything valuable. And tell me, where the heck is there a spot to hide anything in those rooms?"

She pulled out of the garage. The entrance had been shoveled, but when she went to pull out onto the road, it was a mess. The snowplows hadn't cleared the road yet. "I hope all the roads aren't like this."

Snow still fell steadily, the flakes melting instantly on the heated windshield.

"Well, maybe that'll keep the perps indoors," Shep said. "Where are you going?"

"To the diner first. I'm hungry, and I need a coffee."

"Sounds like a plan. Do we have enough time?"

"I hope so. But if we're a bit late, the weather is a good excuse."

It was impossible to park anywhere close to the diner. Shep suggested, "Just drop me off, and I'll get us a coffee and some food. What do you want?"

"I'll have a cheese muffin and a caramel macchiato. I'll pay next time. It'll be a long night. I hate these twelve-hour shifts." She dropped him off in front of the diner. "I'll drive around the block."

By the time she got back, he was already outside waiting for her and quickly got into the car. He set the coffee in the holder and unwrapped the muffin for her. "Here you go," he said.

"Thanks."

It didn't take as long as expected to get to the precinct. Arnia parked the vehicle and sipped the last of her coffee. "That feels better," she murmured and put the empty container in the trash.

"I'll say. Do you mind waiting a few minutes? I need to

shave, remember?"

"I have to clock in anyway and put on my vest and uniform jacket, but don't be too long. We're not that early. I took my time driving."

To her surprise, Captain Schmidt was still there. "Powell, in my office for a minute, please. How are the roads?" he asked while she followed him into the office.

"Main roads are slushy. Snow's still coming down hard."

"How was your first experience with Daniels? Notice anything strange about the guy?"

"No, sir. What am I supposed to be looking for?"

He shrugged. "Captain Hinkelmann of the Langley precinct warned me that the man has shown some odd behavior."

"Odd? How? Need I be afraid of him?"

"No, I don't think so. Hinkelmann didn't elaborate. If anything makes you uncomfortable, come to me right away."

"I will. It's early days. We've got a week of nights. That'll give me time to get to know my new partner."

"Should be quiet. I doubt even the perps and little hoodlums venture out in this weather."

"True, the streets are quiet. Goodnight, Captain."

Arnia hurried to her locker to put on her vest, duty belt, and police jacket. Shep was already there waiting for her. "Have you clocked in?" she asked.

"Yup. You ready to roll?"

"It doesn't look like this snow is letting up any time soon," Arnia commented as they began patrolling the East End.

"Good. That'll make for quiet nights."

They drove slowly through the streets and alleys. As predicted, there were barely any pedestrians out on the streets. In the alleys, the homeless hovered around burning oil barrels, trying to keep warm. Looking at them, especially the young children hovering close to their parents, made her heart ache.

After driving around for a few hours, she pulled up near a street vendor. Arnia was surprised to see the cart. Bert sold hot dogs, soup, and popcorn. But surely business was bad right now… "I could stand some hot soup. What about you?" she asked Shep.

"Yes, and a hot dog. Is it safe? I mean…the guy looks kind of ragged, and —"

"I've bought his food for the last four years. His clothes might be tattered, but he's clean, and the food has never made me sick. My turn to buy. How many hot dogs?"

"Two, please, loaded."

She left the car running and quickly went to the cart. "Hi, Bert. I'm surprised to see you out here in this weather."

"Gotta make a living, Arnia. Night shift?"

"Yup. Three loaded hot dogs and two soups. What kind did you brew this time?"

"Pea soup with real sausage."

"Business can't be that good in this weather," Arnia said while she waited.

"It hasn't been too bad. I have to charge more for the soup, but it's damn popular. Here you go." Bert handed her two containers filled with steaming soup.

Just the steam coming from them made Arnia's mouth water. She hadn't had pea soup in a long time. She quickly took the soup to the car and then returned for the hot dogs, spoons, and napkins. She paid Bert and gave him a bigger-than-usual tip. Bert's Hot Dog and Soup Cart did quite well, but she knew he merely lived in a tent in an alley.

"Got a new partner, I see," Bert noted.

"Yes. Scott's been transferred."

"Have a good night. See you tomorrow, Arnia."

She hurried back to the car with the hot dogs, handed them to Shep, and then got into the driver's seat.

"This soup is to die for," Shep said.

"Yes, he cooks up some good stuff. I'll go park somewhere so we can eat in peace."

She drove to a quiet alley and parked. After they had finished their food, they continued their patrol. Everything was quiet until they drove past one of the nightclubs. Even during a snowstorm, nightlife continued... The muffled sound of music thumped through the walls.

A group of men and women stood outside the club, watching a fight between several men that had spilled from the club onto the snow-covered street. The air was thick with the sound of shouted slurs and the sharp smacks of fists. Arnia briefly turned on her siren and pulled up. She and Shep got out of the vehicle and made their way through the jeering crowd. The siren had not stopped the fight nor scattered the bystanders.

"What's going on here?" Arnia shouted at one of the women who stood shivering in a scanty mini dress that had a plunging neckline exposing half her breasts, the nipples almost popping out. She wore thigh-high boots, about the only item of clothing that'd help against the deep snow. Except for the six-inch spiked heels...

"Gordie, the guy with red hair, hit on Susan. Her boyfriend attacked Gordie. The other dude is Gordie's friend," the woman told her.

In a blur of movement, Shep intervened — and something shifted. The moment one of the men's fists connected with Shep's jaw, the air itself seemed to charge. The chain around her neck vibrated eerily and felt unusually warm.

His eyes...

They glowed...

A molten, fiery orange...

She blinked, her heart pounding. Had she imagined it?

He tore the men apart and sent them flying into different

directions, his strength unnerving. There was no hesitation. Just raw, unrelenting power.

Arnia's heart pounded as she gazed at Shep's face while he dealt with the three men. His eyes glowed, but the glow disappeared once he separated the guys. She shook her head, trying to make sense of what she'd just witnessed. He was much stronger than what he'd displayed before at the shooting incident...

And his eyes...

It had not been her imagination.

They had glowed.

Arnia swallowed hard, her breath ragged. Whatever she'd just seen, it wasn't normal. And she needed to find out exactly who Shepherd Daniels really was.

Was this what the captain was talking about? For now, there was no way she was going to report the strange incident. Tucking it away for the moment, she joined him in warning the men. They were quite inebriated.

"What do we do? Take them in?" Shep said close to her ear.

Cologne... He must have used aftershave after he'd shaved. It smelled fresh, almost intoxicatingly so. "Let's see if any of them are driving. If so, we'll take the keys. They can pick them up at the station tomorrow. I don't think the guys are drunk enough to throw them in the tank."

"Sure we shouldn't throw them in the tank anyway? They'll be back at it soon as we leave," Shep said.

"Which one of you ladies is Susan?" Arnia called out to the women.

A young woman with spiked green hair and scantily dressed stepped forward. "That's me."

"Any of these guys drive here?"

Susan shook her head. "Can't afford a car. We walked."

"Are you telling me the truth?" But Arnia knew that she was... The nightclub was a dive, a place for homeless troublemakers to hang out.

"No cars, Officer. I promise," Susan said.

"Okay. We're letting you off easy this time, but watch it. We'll be back to check on you lot," she warned the men who stood sheepishly waiting.

"You're too soft, Arnia," Shep told her as she pulled away from the nightclub.

"Maybe. The world is already harsh enough without making it worse." She drove silently for a bit, her mind on what had just happened, until she came to a quiet alley almost clear of homeless people. She pulled into it and parked.

"What are you doing?" Shep asked.

"I need to talk to you." She unclasped her belt and turned to face him. "What happened back there?"

"Arnia, you're not making any sense. You know what happened."

"Bullshit. You displayed strength unlike anything I've ever seen. And your eyes glowed."

He gave her a lopsided grin. "You told me you have books. You've read too many fantasy stories."

"Don't screw with me, Shep. I know what I saw. You'd better tell me, or I'll have no choice but to talk to the captain. Are you some kind of augmented super-soldier? I know that ever since the alien invasion, scientists have been experimenting, creating human-looking androids capable of fighting the aliens should they ever return. I've seen pictures of them. They look uncannily real."

"I'm not an android."

Well…damn. He's almost too perfect for a normal guy… His body is flawless and chiseled to perfection… Did they really discover how to make androids that are almost like humans? But why would he be working as an ordinary cop? His skin feels real. And he grows a beard and all. He's lying about something. There is something not natural about Shepherd Daniels.

"I'm going to be honest with you, Shep. I expect you to be just as honest with me. Captain Schmidt asked me to watch for anything strange I notice about you or your behavior. It appears that the captain of the Langley precinct warned Schmidt that something is off about you."

He was quiet for a bit, then gazed into her eyes. "I'll be as honest with you as I can. But not here. Not right now. Can you wait until after our shift?"

"I suppose."

"Please don't tell the captain anything."

"I'll wait to decide that until after we've talked."

CHAPTER SEVEN

They returned to the station at five-thirty in the morning to type up their report. Arnia recorded the fight at the nightclub, but she didn't mention anything about the strange phenomenon she had witnessed.

Not yet…

First, she needed to hear what Shep had to say.

Who was he?

What was he?

And then she would make up her mind whether or not to report any of it to Schmidt.

Just after six, she clocked out. She took her backpack out of her locker and threw her dirty uniform in the hamper. Thankfully, the precinct looked after the cleaning of their uniforms once a week. Shep was already done and waited for her in the locker room, a duffel bag in his hand.

"Can we stop somewhere quiet? A restaurant, maybe? We can have some breakfast while we talk," he suggested.

"There's only the diner on the way home. Remember, I can't take the car anywhere else."

"Well, not the coziest of places, but I guess we can sit there."

"At least the food is good. And it's warm."

The plows could hardly keep up with the snow, and even the main roads were difficult to drive on. If it didn't stop snowing soon, Arnia knew she'd have to put chains on the tires, something she didn't really want to do. Then again, she had a strong man with her who could do it for her.

A very strong man...

Unusually so...

Trust me to fall for an android...

She shook the thought from her mind and glanced at him, the reddish stubble on his face, his handsome, angular profile... Nope, he couldn't be. He was too real. Neither could they have augmented him after an accident... There wasn't a scar on his body, and she'd seen all of him... Naked, he was perfection, a living sculpture... Had he ever been in the army? It was one of the questions she'd ask him later.

The diner was quiet. Most people would still be in bed. "Coffee?" Shep asked.

She nodded. "Yes, please. And a cheese muffin?"

"How about eggs? You need your protein."

"I had a hot dog, remember?"

"I'd hardly call that healthy protein."

"Just a muffin, please."

It didn't take long. They were the only customers so far. Shep set the coffee and muffin on the table, then slid into the booth opposite her. She sipped the hot brew first. "Okay, begin talking. Or wait...let me ask you something first. Were you ever a soldier? In the army?"

He gave her that endearing lopsided grin. "Nope. Always a cop. Why?"

"Okay, start talking. I'm listening."

He took a deep breath. "First of all, I think fate has brought us together. Or...not fate. The pendants."

"Wh-what?"

"You've only had yours for a little while. But have you felt anything at all? A vibration of any kind coming from it?"

"Eh...yes." Where was he going with this? Wasn't the static that she felt when touching the necklace just from the cold weather? Just like her hair became staticky? But there was the way it had vibrated and gotten hot when Shep had jumped in to separate the fighting guys at the club...

"Okay. Let me start at the beginning. I'm adopted. I was a newborn foundling, only wearing the chain and pendant when my parents discovered me in a hollow tree. When—"

"What the hell? How is that possible? I mean—"

"You want me to explain, so stop interrupting.

"Sorry." She picked up her coffee and sipped it to avoid interrupting him again.

"Twenty-five years ago, a young man and woman were hiking in Oregon's Valley of the Giants. Have you ever been there?"

"No, but I've seen pictures of it. Humongous trees."

"Right. The couple heard strange sounds coming from one of the trees, a hollow tree. When they checked it out, they found a newly born naked baby boy and the necklace. Namely, me. The umbilical cord was fresh, so they figured the mother must still be around. They wrapped me in one of their jackets and searched, but didn't find a woman who could have given birth to me. They didn't find anyone. They ended up hiking back to Falls City, where they were told to take me to Dallas, where they took me to the fire department. The Fire Chief called the Polk County Sheriff's Office, which contacted CPS. CPS came and picked me up and took me to a hospital. I believe efforts were made to try to locate the woman who must have given birth to me. But I ended up in an orphanage."

"So, how did you end up in Vancouver?" Arnia asked when he stopped for a bit to drink his coffee.

"The couple who initially found me, who later became my mom and dad, somehow kept track of what happened to me. They were newlyweds, and when my mother found out that I was in an orphanage, she talked to my father, and they decided to adopt me. My father was a cop who was killed in action when I was five. Mom had the twins when I was three, and she was originally from Vancouver. When she was widowed so young with three kids, she decided to go back to Vancouver to live with her parents, who owned a house there."

"When they found you, you had the chain and pendant around your neck?"

"Yes. Mom kept it safe for me until I was a teenager, when she gave it to me and finally told me I was adopted."

"That still doesn't explain the strange phenomenon you displayed last night."

"Let me get to that. But I want another coffee first."

The diner was filling up quickly. Some were there to get coffee and takeout, and a few others were now occupying the other booths. It took Shep a little while to return to their booth. He set her coffee on the table and sipped his first before continuing.

"It didn't take me long to begin feeling the strange currents and vibrations coming from the chain. I think I was around sixteen when I began feeling different. Because of my speed and strength, I excelled in sports in school and later at the academy. I still didn't connect it to the necklace. And the first time I became aware of my X-ray eyes, as I call them, was when I got into a fight at a bar and got punched in the face. The necklace became super-hot, so much that it felt scalding. The fight was all over the young woman I was with. The fury within me caused me to pick up the other guy and toss him through the bar like a tennis ball. The police came, causing most of the people to scatter like scared rabbits and leave the bar. The woman, Monica, told me afterward that my eyes glowed orange and that laser beams shot from them. It was only then that I began connecting it all to the necklace."

"But you were a cop. How much trouble did you get into?

And did Monica tell the other cops about your eyes?"

"I didn't get into trouble. I knew the guys. They were from my precinct, and I told them that the other man was getting fresh with my girl. All I ended up with was a stiff warning from the captain. That was in Toronto. Monica didn't tell them about my eyes, but she broke up with me. She said she was scared, that there was something really weird about me."

"But how did you end up being a cop in Toronto?"

"After I finished school, I left home and made my way to Ontario. That's where I enrolled in the academy."

"Do you think that your extra strength and glowing eyes are caused by the pendant?"

"Yes, I've known that ever since that fight. You haven't had yours long enough. But maybe it wasn't yours to begin with. You got it after your mother passed? Did she always have it? Did she ever display any strange phenomena?"

"No. I didn't even know she had it. She hid it well for all those years. After we finish our coffee, we'll go home to my room. There's something I want to show you."

"You didn't report any of what you saw, did you?"

"Nope. I wanted to talk to you first."

"I've fought against the strangeness so hard, and I've been careful not to get into fights, but as a cop, it can't be helped sometimes. Not long before the transfer to Vancouver, I had to get physical with a gang of hooligans. I think one of my fellow officers saw my eyes glowing, noticed my strength, and reported it. I believe that's one of the reasons I got transferred."

"Do you think the pendant has magical powers or something?"

He shrugged. "I don't know. I've thought about not wearing it, but it's valuable, and I'm too afraid of losing it. You warned me that the rooms get broken into quite often. Where could I keep it where it's safe?"

"In the safe at the precinct?"

"That's a possibility I haven't thought of."

After arriving back at their building, Arnia took him to her room. She dug up one of the books from under the mattress, took out the envelope with her mother's letter, and handed it to him. "Read this." She sat on the bed, drew up her knees, and indicated for him to take the wobbly chair, watching his face as he began reading.

After a minute, the letter sank to his knees, and he looked at her, his eyes one big question mark. For moments, he held her gaze, realization sinking in, before he continued to read. When he was done, he folded the letter carefully and put it back into the envelope. "There's no way we can be related."

It was a statement, not a question. She shook her head and giggled. "Hardly. I'm black, and you're very white."

"But it can't be a coincidence. Both of us wearing the same necklace and found in a hollow tree? How old are you?"

"Twenty-three. I've given it a bit of thought. The only thing I can come up with is that we were both part of some experiment. But why were we left inside trees? That one is a mystery. If we hadn't been found, we would have died within days. It makes me wonder if there were any other babies left to die inside hollow trees in that forest."

"With chains and pendants around their necks?" he said with a smirk.

"I know. It's more than probably a mystery we'll never solve."

"Like my glowing eyes…"

"Yes, and your super strength. Could it be that they were experimenting on babies?"

"Possible, but why hide us in hollow trees? And we were newly born. We still had the umbilical cord."

"Maybe the mothers were experimented on? The mothers escaped and gave birth in the forest. But why leave us there?

Why the chains and the pendants? Is it the necklace that gives you the extra powers? I wish we had access to government websites. If only I knew a hacker… We should investigate if there are any science institutes in the vicinity of that forest."

"The chain and pendant get very hot, and it vibrates whenever my strength surfaces," Shep told her.

"I've only had my necklace a short while. The only thing I've noticed so far is that it gets staticky, and it's strange, but it vibrated and got warm when you were in that fight at the nightclub. But I blamed the static on the below-zero weather, just like my hair gets staticky. Does that mean I'll have a weird phenomenon, too, after I've worn it for a while?"

"Only time will tell, I guess."

"One thing I can promise you, I won't breathe a word about any of it to Schmidt. I'm sure glad I didn't include it in my report of the incident at the nightclub."

"And I can tell you one thing for sure, too…" He stood and, in one step, reached and pulled her off the bed and into his arms. He tilted her chin and gazed into her eyes. "You and I are connected. I felt it the moment I met you. And now I'm surer than ever. We belong together."

Arnia held her breath, her heart hammering against her ribs. When he bent and his lips tenderly touched hers, she thought her heart would jump out of her chest. This felt so right.

She melted into him, her hands tracing the firm line of his shoulders. His arms tightened around her, pulling her even closer. The taste of him was intoxicating, and so was the heat, the tenderness, and the spark that danced between them. Time slipped away, leaving only the two of them entwined in the moment.

Whatever mysteries still lingered, whatever truths remained hidden, they could wait…

His lips claimed hers once more, this time deeper, more

urgent. She wound her fingers through his hair, tugging him closer as he lowered her to the bed. The wooden frame creaked beneath their weight, and the world around them faded away as his fingers traced the contours of her face and tangled in her hair.

But then the shadows of the unknown crept back in, the chains around their necks, the unanswered questions. But every kiss, every touch, pushed the uncertainty far away…

Today, right now, there was no past, no future…

*

Hours later, Arnia stirred, the warmth of Shep's body still wrapped around her. His arm draped protectively over her waist, his breathing steady. She traced the edge of his jaw, memorizing the shape of his face. But the unanswered questions still gnawed at her. What if the pendants weren't just relics of the past? What if they were something more? Something dangerous? Sinister?

Shep's eyelids flickered open. He pulled her closer, pressing a kiss on her forehead. "We fell asleep," he said huskily.

"We did. Understandably. A long night and an emotional early morning… It's three-thirty."

He kissed her gently, then sat up. "I guess it's time to get ready for work."

"Yes. Although it feels like we just got back from last night's shift…"

He leaned down and kissed her again. "You're still troubled. Not to worry. We'll find answers."

"I don't know how or where. For now, we'd best get a move on." She sat on her knees and looked down at the street. "Oh my! There has to be four feet of snow. And the road hasn't been plowed."

"Well, hopefully, they'll plow it very soon, or we won't be able to get to the precinct. Then again, I wouldn't mind spending the night here..."

She got off the bed. If he spent the night, a lot more than just kissing and cuddling would happen... But everything was happening too fast. She wasn't ready to give herself completely to him. Not yet...even if she longed for him to make love to her...

CHAPTER EIGHT

All Arnia could do was slowly follow the snowplow until they got to the main road, which was hopefully cleared—or...mostly cleared and salted. At the rate it continued to snow, the plows wouldn't be able to keep up with it soon.

"Patrolling in this is going to be fun," Shep muttered.

"Yes, I've never experienced a winter like it."

"Global warming."

"That's what they blame everything on. Feels more like an ice age setting in."

"Heaven forbid."

"I saw an old movie about just such a scenario a long time ago when I still lived at the Rivera house. And then it all began to melt, and flooding happened," Arnia said.

"I suppose there's no internet connection in our rooms?"

"Nope. And I've never invested in a laptop. I'd have to take it to work with me all the time. Wouldn't be safe in my room. Plus, without connection, what's the use? There are only a few internet cafes, and they're damn expensive."

"I've got a laptop. It's in my bag."

"Which is in your room. I suggest you bring it to work and keep it in your locker there before it gets stolen."

"We have to clock in each shift anyway, so I may just carry it to work every day, keep it in my locker, and then take it back home again at the end of my shift."

"Why have it in your room if you can't access the internet?"

"I can."

"How?"

"A guy I know in Langley told me how. He also showed me how to access the dark web. I'm going to start researching our pendants."

"It also means you'll have to carry it with you wherever you go, even on your days off."

"I know and don't care. It fits inside my backpack. Though it's rather a nuisance. The room I had in Langley, I didn't have to worry about thieves. It was a lot safer."

"Again, you were lucky there to have had a room in a private residence. I'm surprised you haven't researched the necklace before now."

"It's because of yours and everything we talked about that I'm really curious now."

"Maybe you should also research babies found in hollow trees. It could be that we weren't the only ones left there."

"You could be right, and over a period of some years, because I'm more than two years older than you."

"The thought that I could be a product of some experiment gives me the creeps," she said softly.

"Make that both of us."

"Have you discussed any of it with your mother at all?" she wondered.

"No. What I said before when you asked why I didn't live with my family... I lied. Mom doesn't live in a house or a room. She lives on the streets. After my father was killed, she turned to alcohol and drugs. Thankfully, when we were kids, we lived with my grandparents, who looked after us. Mom was gone most of the time. Occasionally, she came home and promised us the world. But she never lasted longer than a day or two. She broke her parents' hearts. My sisters got married very young, and as you know, I left and went to Ontario and entered the police academy there. Not long after I was gone, my grandparents both died within a year of each other. They left Mom the house, which she promptly sold on a whim for far below its value, and she wasted the money on drugs, alcohol, and whatever else. She lived in a room for a while, but then she took to the streets. We've tried to help her, but she wants nothing to do with any of us."

"I'm so sorry, Shep. Do you visit your sisters?"

"Sometimes."

"Your mother is in Vancouver somewhere?"

"Yes. In the alleys. I need to find her to see how she's doing in this horrible weather. But it's like looking for a phantom. She uses fake names and shifts from one alley to another. She is the main reason I came back to British Columbia. It was really hard when I was stationed in Langley, but now that I'm in Vancouver, maybe it'll be easier to keep an eye out for her. My sisters have given up on her and have pretty much disowned her."

"We can watch for her while we're patrolling the East End. What does she look like?"

"The last time I saw her was about three weeks ago. She's shaved her head. She has brown eyes, is short, and very thin. I don't have a picture of her."

"What is her real name?"

"Maureen Daniels. But she always changes her name to hide from us, which makes it very difficult to find her, as I already told you."

"And now you have me to help you. Thank you for trusting me with such private information."

They finally arrived at the precinct. Captain Schmidt greeted them after they clocked in. "Well, I'm glad you two made it. We're heavily understaffed, thanks to the weather. I'm not even going to try going home yet."

"Understandable. The plows can barely keep up," Arnia

answered.

"Prepare yourselves for chaos. There'll be a lot more accidents, and the weather won't stop the gangs and young hoodlums. Dispatch can hardly keep up with the calls coming in."

"How many cars on patrol tonight?" Shep asked.

"Besides yours, two are occupied with a twelve-car pileup on the Knight Street bridge right now. You're the Lone Ranger until they get that mess cleared up."

Arnia went to the locker room, Shep on her heels. "Schmidt is more friendly than usual," she said over her shoulder while taking her vest and belt out of her locker and putting them on. "Ready? Let's go play in the snow."

A fierce gale greeted them as they drove out of the underground parking lot. Thankful for heated windows, Arnia leaned forward, peering at the road. The snow was so thick, she could barely see where they were going.

"I wonder how many homeless are going to survive this," she murmured, too late remembering that Shep's mother was one of them.

She drove slowly down East Hastings toward Gastown, checking out alleys, but Shep saw no sign of his mother.

There were virtually no pedestrians and very few vehicles on the road. When she came to what was commonly known as Crack Alley, between Columbia and Carral, she turned into it. It was the alley where many addicts hung out, and many drug deals went down. The graffiti-covered walls gave some color to the dismal scene. It was possible that his mother was hanging out there.

Garbage containers stood against the walls, homeless people huddling between them beneath old tarps, cut-up cardboard boxes, and sheets of plastic. She knew that most of the bins would be occupied by addicts and the homeless seeking shelter from the severe cold.

"Where is this?" Shep asked.

"The locals call it Crack Alley. This is where many of the addicts hang out. I'm surprised you don't know about it."

"There are so many alleys filled with homeless souls. And though I am originally from Vancouver, we lived in the West End. I'm not familiar with this area at all."

"This one is the worst. A lot of drug deals go down here." She didn't want to add that a lot of bodies were removed on an almost daily basis.

"Look at that," he exclaimed, pointing at a woman trying to climb into a container, but whoever was already in it kept pushing her out. She fell to the ground but doggedly got back up and continued trying to get into it.

"The garbage bins provide shelter if they're lucky enough to grab one," Arnia told him.

He grunted. "Can't imagine sleeping with all that filth."

"Beats freezing to death, I guess," she answered grimly.

"This alley is long enough."

"Yup."

"Unless we're on foot, I wouldn't be able to find my mother among all these people. That's if she's here."

"Not a good idea. Walking in Crack Alley at night is deadly dangerous." She stomped on the brake.

"What are you doing?"

"You don't see that body in the snow right in front of the car?"

"Yes, now that I really look. It's covered in snow. Dead?"

Arnia opened the door and stepped out. Snow bit into her cheeks. The wind flipped her hair, so she could hardly see. Quickly, she bunched it up into a knot, then groped for her flashlight.

Carefully, she approached the immobile figure almost buried by snow. But he or she didn't move, not even when she began to remove some of the snow to reveal a man with a dark beard, maybe in his mid-forties. His eyes were open, glazed. The hilt of a dagger protruded from his chest. She felt for a pulse. "Nothing," she told Shep, who had joined her. "Call it in."

"You sure he's dead?" Shep asked.

"Just slightly. He's got a knife in his chest. The man's been lying here for a while. He's frozen." She heard Shep call it in while she crouched next to the dead man. He'd been murdered. But from experience, she knew it wouldn't be treated the same as a regular murder scene. The coroner would come to pick up the body. No detectives would show up... There would be no investigation.

"Get back in the car while we wait," Shep called out to her. "You'll freeze to death."

"Hey, use your laser eyes. Maybe you can conjure up a warming field around us," she tried to joke.

"That's not funny," Shep snapped.

He'd joined her. She looked up at him. "Sorry."

"Could be a while before the coroner gets here. We should wait in the vehicle."

Absentmindedly, she nodded. "Lord knows how many other dead bodies are here." She heard a rustling behind her and swiveled to look. A woman in rags, a tattered blanket around her head and upper body, came crawling from behind a makeshift cardboard shelter.

"His name is Spot."

"Is it? And what is your name?"

"Dolly Parton. What's yours?"

"Right. I'm Whitney Houston. Well, Dolly, did you see who killed this man?"

"Didn't see fuckin' nothing."

It was possible that the woman hadn't seen anything. But Arnia pressed on. "It happened right in front of your space. Tell me, Dolly, or I'll have to take you in."

The woman began to shuffle back and tried to pull the cardboard over herself, but Shep was faster. He took the woman by the arm and pulled her to stand up.

"Answer the officer," he ordered.

"He was already dead when I got here," the woman muttered.

"Forget it, Shep. We never get anywhere with these people," Arnia told him. "Let her go."

He didn't. Instead, he asked, "Do you know a woman called Maureen Daniels? A woman with no hair?"

"Baldi? She croaked more than a week ago. Let me go."

Shep let go so suddenly that the woman almost fell. Cursing, she climbed back beneath the cardboard shelter. Just then, the coroner arrived on the scene.

They wasted no time. Arnia and Shep answered a few questions, and after the coroner left, they got back into the cruiser. "Do you want to look further down this alley?" Arnia asked.

"Didn't you hear what that woman said?"

"Yes, but can you believe her? Baldi? Really?"

"It's possible. How many bald homeless women are there? I guess I'll have to go to the morgue tomorrow morning to see if it's true," he said somberly. "That's if the body is still there."

CHAPTER NINE

The night went by fast. They were dispatched to several accidents, a break-in, and a domestic dispute, and finally, their shift was over. "I just realized we haven't eaten anything all night," Arnia told Shep while taking off her vest and duty belt.

"We've hardly had time. Before anything, I'd like to go to the morgue. Where is it?"

"Vancouver General Hospital on West Twelfth Avenue. We'll go there first. After we pick up a coffee."

"Is it out of our way? The mileage—"

"I doubt the captain will care right now. The weather can account for extra mileage. That woman might not have been telling the truth," she warned Shep. "How long ago did your mom shave her hair?"

"Not sure. I didn't ask when I saw her last. She told me it was easier to take care of and stopped her getting lice."

"How often did you see her?"

"I made a point of going to Vancouver at least once a month, but I couldn't always find her."

"When was the last time you saw her with hair?"

He frowned. "Mm, I think at least eight months ago or more. Before that, a couple of times she had a rag wound around her head. Why?"

"For her to have the nickname Baldi... If that is indeed her."

The first thing Arnia did was stop to pick up coffee. She

gratefully drank the hot brew while cautiously driving to the hospital. Shep was very quiet. She wondered what was going through his mind. She admired him for still caring about his mother and not abandoning her like his sisters had done.

"For lack of a name, we'll call that woman Dolly... Dolly probably has no idea of the timeframe either. To the homeless, one day flows into the next. And if they're addicts, they completely lose all track of time. Dolly could be wrong about the death of the bald woman."

"You're trying to make this easier on me," Shep said while she parked.

It took them a while to get information on the unidentified deceased who had arrived in the morgue in the last two weeks before a nurse accompanied them to the morgue, which was in the basement. Only three of the recent deceased were women between the ages of approximately fifty and seventy.

The first two had hair, and the third was bald. Arnia could immediately tell by Shep's expression that this was his mother. "I'm sorry," she told him softly.

He looked at the nurse. "Yes, this is her. Her name is Maureen Daniels." His voice cracked, and he cleared his throat. "What do I do now?"

"Go upstairs to the administration office to do the paperwork. You'll need to make arrangements with a funeral home, Officer."

Arnia gazed at the still body. A sheet covered her up to her neck. The face was very pale and so very thin, the cheeks sunken, her lips very thin and also sunken, indicating she'd lost all her teeth.

"Cause of death?" Shep asked the nurse.

"Overdose. I'm sorry, Officer."

"When did she come in?"

"Three days ago."

"At least she's out of her misery," he mumbled and turned

away from the sight of the remains. He groped for Arnia's hand. "Let's go upstairs to administration to do the paperwork."

She squeezed his hand. "You can get time off, you know, to make the arrangements and all. It's paid compassionate leave."

"I don't need time off. There won't be a funeral or anything. She had no friends. I'll make arrangements to have her cremated."

"Shouldn't you consult your sisters?" she asked carefully.

"I doubt they care."

"Maureen is their mother, too. They must still have some feelings for her."

He shrugged. "I doubt it, but I'll call them after we leave here."

The paperwork didn't take long. Shep needed to contact a funeral home that would take care of the rest. "Let's go get some breakfast," he suggested while they drove along Twelfth Avenue.

They stopped at the first diner they came to. It was very quiet. Only one customer sat in one of the booths. Arnia slid into a booth while Shep ordered their breakfast and bought coffee.

He slid into the booth opposite her. His face was pale and drawn.

"You okay, Shep?" Arnia asked worriedly.

"Yes. Sad. Such a wasted life."

"There must have been good days... Try and think about those and not what became of her." Arnia didn't know what else to say.

Shep took his phone out of his pocket. "I'd better call my sisters."

Arnia sipped her coffee while he made the first call. She only heard his side of the conversation, but it wasn't good.

Very short.

"Tasha, it's me. I found Mom. She's gone. Died a few days ago, and—"

He lowered the phone and stared at it. "She hung up on me."

"Oh, Shep… I'm so sorry. I don't know what to say."

"I don't even know if I want to call my other sister now."

"You have to."

He stared at her for a moment, then nodded and dialed a number. "Rachel, it's Shep. I just came from the hospital. It's Mom."

He listened for a few minutes.

"No, she's not sick. She died, Rachel. A few days ago. I'll make arrangements today to have her cremated. That's if it's okay with you. Tasha didn't want to talk. She hung up on me."

It was another much-too-brief conversation. "What did she say?" Arnia asked.

"She's leaving it all in my hands. Like Tasha, she doesn't really care, but Rachel is at least somewhat sad, mostly at my mother's wasted life. The girls don't remember anything about the time when my father was still alive. I was five when he died, and I remember happier days, when she was still a sweet and loving mother. I'm also grateful that she and my dad rescued me from that tree. I would have died there if they hadn't found me. But the girls don't know about that. They don't even know that I was adopted."

"Should you tell them? It might soften their feelings toward Maureen."

He looked thoughtful for a few moments, then shook his head. "No, I don't think so. Natasha can be hard. It could change her feelings toward me, too. It's better they continue believing I'm their real brother."

In a way, Arnia understood. He didn't want to lose the

connection with the only family he had left… She had so often wished for some family…even an aunt or uncle, a cousin or two… But she had no one. As far as she knew, according to the letter, her mother was an orphan who had no family when she'd made her way to Vancouver. "I never knew I was adopted until I read my mother's letter. Or that she found me in a tree."

He gave her a wry grin. "The tree foundlings. Almost sounds like the title of a book or a movie."

"I still wonder if we were the only ones who were left there. I can't wait for you to do some research on your laptop to see if there's a science institute in the vicinity of that forest."

Shep had been looking for something on his phone. "Found a funeral home not far from the hospital. I'll call it now." He made the call, and after a brief conversation and explanation, he hung up and looked at her. "You heard. I have to go there to sign release papers and pay for the cremation. Maybe you can drop me off on your way home?"

"I'll go with you."

"We have to work at six. You'll be exhausted. I'll be fine on my own."

"No. I'm going with you," she said firmly. She was all he had. He was very much alone in this, and it weighed on him. She could tell.

"I guess you had to deal with the same not that long ago," he suddenly said. "You told me your mother passed just recently."

"A few months ago, and yes, when I located her in an alley, she was very close to death. I didn't know how sick she was. I only saw her once a month, and the last time I was with her, she coughed a lot and said she still had a very bad cold. I didn't know that she was already living on the streets. The rich woman she worked for had kicked her out."

"And she didn't say anything?"

"No. If she had, I would have taken her to a clinic and had her live with me."

"She didn't want to burden you."

"I guess. Mom didn't show up the next month when I went to the diner where we usually met. I was worried and went to the Rivera estate, and the woman told me that she'd terminated Mom's employment some months before." Arnia stopped for a moment and swallowed hard. "Terminated is a nice word for kicking someone out on the street."

"I gather your mother didn't see a doctor."

"No. She kept saying she had a cold. I bought cough medicine for her that she took. She probably didn't go to the clinic because if diagnosed with TB, the medication costs a fortune. It's not free anymore. And I suspect she knew what was wrong with her. I would have paid for her meds. By the time I found her in the alley, it was too late. At least I got to say goodbye to her."

"I'm so sorry."

When they got home, it was after lunch. "We'd better get a few hours' sleep," Shep told her. "I'm so thankful that you stuck with me."

She squeezed his hand, then stood on her tiptoes and kissed him briefly. "Always. We're partners. That doesn't stop after work. I'll see you at four at the car."

Arnia quickly took off her clothes and wrapped the thin blanket around her before relaxing on the bed. Though she was really tired, sleep didn't come easily. The events of that day haunted her mind, and when she finally focused on other things, the questions about her and Shep's origin and how similar their circumstances were began to resurface…

Both were found in a hollow tree…

Two-and-a-half years apart…

There was no way they could be related…

But there had to be a connection…

CHAPTER TEN

Arnia rubbed her eyes. It was four p.m. She'd only had a few hours' rest. Her eyes felt as if they had a pound of sand in them. When her vision cleared a bit, she gazed out the window. Thick flakes still tumbled from a heavy sky. Looking down at the street, she saw that it had not yet been plowed, but she saw the snowplow approaching slowly in the distance, followed by a salt truck.

She swung her legs over the side of the bed and stood. Shep was probably already waiting for her... Grabbing her robe and shrugging into it, she quickly ran to the communal bathroom to brush her teeth and wash her face, and then hurried back to get dressed.

"Sorry I'm late," she said, breathing heavily from running.

Shep grinned. "I just got here myself."

"You okay? Did you get any sleep?" she asked while unlocking the car.

"Yes, I tossed for a bit, but then I slept like a log. Waking up wasn't that easy. It's weird. Everything seems like a bad dream now. Unreal."

"I can imagine. To change the subject, I think we need to put the chains on the tires."

"Oh, fun."

She opened the car door and flipped the switch for the trunk. Shep already had the jack and the chains out when she walked to the back of the vehicle. "Wouldn't it be nice if we could just lift the car, huh? You should be able to do that easily with all your extra strength."

"Hercules… Here he comes," he joked, playfully placing his hand under the bumper, pulling a face, and lifting…

Easily!

The car lifted about a foot off the ground!

"What the hell!" he yelled, yanking his hand back, dropping the car.

"You didn't just do that," Arnia muttered. The chain around her neck suddenly vibrated and felt warm. Unconsciously, she reached for it and pulled it free from the collar of her uniform.

It felt quite hot to the touch, and she yanked her hand back. "How is *my* necklace reacting again to *your* display of strength?" she wondered in a soft voice.

Shep stared at her, a soft orange glow still playing in his irises. "I don't know what's going on with us. There's something really weird about these pendants. Mine's very hot."

"And your eyes are glowing again," she told him.

"So are yours."

"Don't be ridiculous. I haven't experienced any strength or whatever."

"I've had the necklace since I was a teenager. Why would it suddenly act weirder than ever now?"

"Maybe it's reacting to mine," Arnia suggested. "Maybe reacting to each other?"

"Right. Newborn infants are found in hollow trees wearing matching magical necklaces. Great line to research. I'd better get these chains on." He promptly placed the jack beneath the car and began cranking it up.

Arnia tucked the pendant and chain away. "I'm not sure we should be wearing these anymore. There is something very strange about them."

"I agree, but what do we do with them without having them stolen?"

"It's the only thing I've got left of my mother," she said in a small voice.

"Except it wasn't your mother's. You had it around your neck when she found you. Just like I was wearing mine. And for your information, I don't believe in paranormal stuff, magic, and whatever. That's all fantasy."

"Shep, I saw you picking up the car as if it weighed nothing. That was *not* my imagination. And what about your glowing eyes? And you just told me that mine glow, too. There's not just something weird with the necklaces, there's something wrong with us. Who are we? Where did we come from? Who or what left us in those trees?"

He finished putting the last chain on and returned the jack to the trunk. "I've got my laptop. Let me quickly research something before we take off."

Arnia got into the vehicle and started it. "I'll warm up the car."

Shep opened his backpack and took out the laptop. She noticed it was quite new and top of the line. He fired it up. "Good. I've got a connection. Here we go."

"What are you typing in?"

"I'm on the dark web and typed 'babies found in hollow trees in Valley of the Giants, Oregon.'"

Arnia giggled. "Right. And what does that bring up?"

"Just articles about that forest and about the giant trees. Nothing about babies. Oh, and some articles about abandoned infants, but not in trees."

"You keep searching while I start driving us to work."

The driveway out of the car park had been cleared, but the road was a mess. She hated having the chains on the car. It was noisy and kind of bumpy. She'd never had to drive one with chains. This was the first time that she ended up being the driver. Scott had always driven. If Shep were more familiar with East Vancouver, she'd gladly hand over the keys to him. "Found anything yet?" she asked while slowly heading to the precinct.

"No. I even did a search for skeletons found in that forest and came up with nothing. Because imagine if your mother hadn't found you, or my parents hadn't found me, we would have died quite fast. A newborn baby wouldn't last very long."

"Maybe there were skeletons, and it wasn't newsworthy enough?"

"Hell, everything ends up on the internet nowadays. Especially on the dark web. Name it, and you can find it."

"Do a search for people with supernatural powers."

He grunted. "Right."

She heard the keys clicking as he typed it in.

"That brings up movie characters, books, comic heroes."

"Keep looking. Or type in people with glowing eyes."

"Again, Superman, the Flash, and more of those characters. I'm scrolling through dozens of answers here, but nothing about ordinary humans with glowing eyes."

"Ordinary people with magical abilities?"

"Uh huh...names of magicians performing in various places, like Vegas."

"I give up."

"I don't think we're going to find any answers on the internet."

"We could leave the necklaces in the safe at work."

"That means asking Schmidt and telling him they're real gold. And he would question how we both own identical solid gold chains and pendants. Wouldn't he find that odd, since you only just became my partner? And how could we afford such jewelry on a cop's salary?"

"I didn't think of that."

"I'm afraid we have to continue wearing them, or at least keep them in our pockets. But that's dangerous, too. We could lose them if we get into a chase or battle of some kind."

Without realizing it, they arrived at the precinct. Arnia parked in the underground car park. Before she switched off the engine, she said, "Hey, maybe you and I were sent to Earth from a dying planet or something, like Superman and Supergirl."

"That's a bit far-fetched. And two-and-a-half years apart?" he said with a chuckle. "It's a mystery, sweetheart, one that we're not going to solve in a hurry."

"If we ever do."

"You two are late," Schmidt growled when they walked into the precinct and clocked in.

"Eh, have you seen the roads?" Arnia couldn't help retorting.

"I know. We're short-staffed again. The phones haven't stopped ringing. I've got exactly one detective who showed up, and of course, there had to be a violent crime today. Two men and a woman, murdered. The crime scene is at a private residence on Yale Street. It's obviously tied to the mob. The house is owned by Antonio Lions, leader of the Liontooth Mob. You two are on the case. Good practice for you, Powell."

Arnia had told Schmidt she wanted to become a detective, but she needed to take extra courses before she could even consider the idea.

"Strange that it got called in. They're very good at hiding their crimes and victims," Arnia commented.

"The victims were shot on the front porch as witnessed by a neighbor who called it in. Detective Anderson is already on the scene. I need you two to question the neighbor who called it in, and maybe some of the other neighbors who could have seen something."

Arnia and Shep went back to the car and drove to Yale

Street as fast as the roads allowed. "The forecast is for continuing snow all week and into the next," Shep told her.

"Great."

They arrived at the address. Even in the bad weather and freezing cold, there were many bystanders on the street. The paparazzi were already there, too. The area had not yet been taped off, seeing that only one detective was on the scene.

"Do you have tape in the trunk?" Shep asked.

"Yes, of course."

They began by removing the spectators from the front yard, and then Shep taped off the area while Arnia went up the steps to the verandah. Two men and a young woman lay in pools of blood near the front door. "Forensics?" she asked the detective.

"On their way. So are the ambulance and coroner, but as you know, the streets are bad."

"How long ago did this happen?"

"About two hours ago."

"Witnesses?"

The detective shook his head. "Whoever called it in isn't here. The folks out there are just sensation seekers."

"The captain said it was a neighbor who called it in. Anyone in the house?"

"No one home. The front door is locked. I think the girl might have been staying here, and she was shot when leaving the house or coming home."

"Captain Schmidt told me Antonio Lions owns the place."

"Then the young woman must be his daughter. Her name is Sophia Lions, according to her ID. She has keys in her hand."

"What about the two guys?"

"Two members of the Liontooth Mob. Makes sense now that I know Antonio owns the place. Both guys were packing, but they didn't get a chance to draw their weapons."

"I guess you haven't been able to talk to the neighbors yet."

"Hardly."

Shep came up the steps. "I talked to a neighbor across the street. Said he saw a red vehicle drive by. Shots were fired from it. It happened very fast. He's the one who called it in."

"So a drive-by shooting. Did he get a plate?"

"Nope."

"Car model?"

"Yes, a red Tesla aircar."

"That's something. Not too many people own one of those."

Arnia knelt by the young woman. She was about eighteen or twenty and very pretty with long, wavy black hair spread out on the deck like a halo. Very dark brown eyes gazed sightlessly up at the overhang. Arnia brushed a few strands of hair off the girl's forehead. A strange feeling coursed through her suddenly as she touched the girl's skin, and she felt the necklace vibrate and get quite warm.

Instantly, a scene played in front of her eyes, almost as if she were watching a movie — the young woman coming up the steps, followed by the two men. She laughed and said something in another language, then took a set of keys out of her pocket and went to the front door. The sound of a vehicle, gunshots, and Arnia saw the red Tesla speeding by, and the girl and men crumpling to the deck.

In a flash, she'd seen the man in the passenger seat of the Tesla, the shooter. He was in his mid-thirties, swarthy, with black hair that was tied back, and he had a long scar running down the side of his face. Just as fast as the scene had played, it was gone again, but the shooter's face was engraved in her mind.

"Arnia?" Shep jolted her out of her thoughts. "Forensics is here. So is the coroner."

"Great. Well, there's nothing much for us to do here now.

I've got everything we need to know. We'll leave you to it, Detective."

They drove away slowly. "You're very quiet, Arnia," Shep said. "I'm surprised you didn't want to talk to any of the other neighbors."

"Not necessary. Something happened that has me puzzled."

"Like what?"

"When I touched the young woman, the necklace and pendant vibrated and got hot, and I saw everything happen as if I were watching a movie. I can describe the shooter. The red Tesla's plates were too mud splattered for me to see the numbers."

"We'll need to go to the precinct so you can look at mug shots."

"It was mob-related. That's a surety. Probably one of the other gangs getting back at Antonio Lions for something. But I'll have to look at mug shots quietly. How can we explain to Schmidt that I know what the shooter looks like?"

"Mm, a white lie is in order. Maybe one of the neighbors saw him and gave us a description."

"That would work."

CHAPTER ELEVEN

The rest of the night, they mostly dealt with weather-related accidents. Before clocking out, Arnia went through the database and looked at dozens of photos of mobsters. "Found the shooter," she told Shep, who was sitting next to her. "Paolo Galliano, a member of the Copper Bulldog gang. I couldn't see the driver clearly."

"Since we're off the clock now, send the information to Schmidt. He'll have Paolo Galliano picked up."

On the way home, Shep said, "You know, Arnia, if the necklaces can help us solve crimes this way, it could be really beneficial."

"True, but how often do we get called to a murder scene? I wish it could show us more about us, how we got left in those trees, and where we came from... I mean, who our real parents were."

"If we even had parents. We could have been engineered," he answered.

"I've read about that. It was against the law to begin with, wasn't it?"

"Yes. A Chinese scientist, He Jiankui, and two collaborators went to jail for three years after genetically altering embryos and implanting them in two women. That was in two thousand eighteen. That's over six hundred years ago. I've read a lot about genetically engineered babies online."

"Really? Why?"

"Oh, I thought it was interesting. Some years ago, I came across an article about it. Though it was against the law in many countries for years, scientists never stopped experimenting. From what I found out, it is now possible to choose your baby's sex, genetic traits, coloring, and more. But it's only available to the wealthy."

"I've never heard or read anything about it."

"It's no longer against the law. The human race is dying, not because of genetic defects but because of all the diseases caused by starvation and poverty. Malnutrition in pregnant women is the leading cause of infants being born with defects. Governments worldwide are in the process of creating a perfect human race by allowing genetic engineering. But only certain men and women qualify to take part—professors, doctors, specialists, etcetera."

"And to hell with the rest of us?"

"Basically. If you look at the many homeless worldwide, the number of bodies removed from the streets on a daily basis—humanity is dying, honey."

"Apparently not all humanity if what you just told me is true."

"Exactly."

"And you came up with the hypothesis that we both could be engineered infants? Then why were we left in those trees?"

"Maybe we were a failed experiment. That's why I haven't mentioned any of this to you until now. It's puzzling."

"Both of us? Two-and-a-half years apart? And both left inside a hollow tree? It's too weird, Shep. And it isn't as if the same woman gave birth to both of us. Look at you and look at me… Then again, you are sculptured perfection."

"Well…thank you for the compliment. But I'm hardly perfect. I'm just a cop. Engineered babies have enhanced learning capabilities and become professors, scientists, and such. And talk about perfection... Look at yourself. You're like a living black Barbie doll. Your figure is perfection, your skin flawless, and then there is your straight, blueish black hair and your unusual dark blue eyes..."

"I could be the product of a white and black couple."

"Or you could have been engineered to look like this. Unless you dye your hair, who has hair that color?"

She pulled into a parking spot near the diner. "I don't dye my hair. And so, why throw us out like trash? We obviously didn't meet the *perfect* standard."

He got out of the car. While they walked to the diner, he said, "Maybe our intelligence didn't measure up?"

"And how can they measure that in newborn infants? There's an empty booth. I'll grab it while you fetch our coffee and something to eat."

"What do you want?"

"Doesn't matter."

Arnia slid into the booth. Everything he'd said ran through her mind. Maybe he was onto something... But how? Why? His hypophysis could explain a lot. Like his beautiful, muscular, perfect body... Not a mark anywhere, not a freckle, blemish, nothing... And now that she thought about it, Shep pointing out that her skin was flawless, she didn't have any marks or blemishes either.

He set her coffee and a cheese muffin and his own on the table before sliding into the booth opposite her. "You're thinking about everything I dumped on you."

"Yes, I'm thinking that you might be onto something with your hypophysis. But it still doesn't explain why we got dumped in the forest. How would they know if a newborn baby is smart or not?"

He shrugged. "Maybe we didn't quite turn out the way they wanted? Expected? I don't know. We're smart enough to have gone through school, the academy, and now I know you're aiming to become a detective. You need brains for that."

"What about you? Have you ever thought about becoming more than just a cop? Did you ever want to be anything else?"

"I've wanted to become a policeman ever since I can remember."

"There is also no explanation for the necklaces and the strange powers they're giving us. Your strength, glowing eyes, and me seeing that murder scene play out… Where did the chains and pendants come from? Who put those around our necks? There are too many variables in this equation."

"I'm going to do more research into engineered babies. I'm sure there's a ton of information about it on the dark web now."

"And see if you can find out if there's a science institute somewhere in the vicinity of that forest. We were left there just after birth. Maybe the mothers escaped?"

"And two different women over a span of two-and-a-half years would just abandon their newborn babies in the same tree? What says we were born the natural way? We could be test-tube babies."

She sipped her coffee before answering that one. "Great, now we're not just engineered, but we were created in petri dishes and grew in bubbles or something."

"You've got the detective mind. Try figure it out," he joked.

She ate her muffin in silence, her brain working overtime. After washing down the last crumbs, she drank the last of her coffee and pushed her empty cup toward him.

"That's telling me you'd like another coffee?" he asked and grinned.

"Obviously. Hurry up. People are waiting for an empty booth."

Sure enough, he stood, tossed their empty cups in the garbage, went to the lineup, and a woman approached Arnia.

"Are you leaving?"

"Eh, no. Sorry. My boyfriend is just getting us another coffee." *Boyfriend…* Had she really called him that?

"Fuckin' cops!" The woman swore again a few times and got back in the lineup.

Most of the people who frequented the diner were office workers and others who had jobs, but some of the homeless somehow managed to get their hands on enough money to buy a coffee. This woman was obviously homeless. She looked and smelled unkempt. Arnia felt sorry for her. She had some cash in her pocket and took it out. "Excuse me, ma'am?"

The woman turned, giving Arnia a dirty look. "What?"

"Here. For you." Arnia pushed the five-dollar bill across the table.

At first, it didn't look like the woman would take it, but then she quickly snatched it and, without a thank you, shoved her way back in the line of people.

Shep returned with their coffee and another muffin for each.

"I'm not hungry anymore. I'll keep it for later."

"That was kind of you to give that woman some cash. I never carry any."

"Neither do I. I found it on the street.

"Did you come up with anything while you were waiting?"

"Nothing much…except that it's possible that whoever created us wasn't happy with the results and maybe was ready to get rid of us? And a kindhearted scientist took pity on us and took us out of the laboratory and placed us in the trees?"

"A bit farfetched, especially since it was a few years apart, but anything is possible, I guess. But abandoning us in a huge forest inside hollow trees for wild animals to find us? I doubt it was with the intent for a kind person to find us. How many people go hiking there anymore?"

"Your parents did. And my mother walked through it… And whoever left us there might have done so to save us from a worse fate, with the intention of coming back later to get us. Could it have been the same person?"

"And after the first baby went missing, he or she would try again two-and-a-half years later? No, I don't think so. We're grasping at straws."

"Like I asked you several times before, look on your laptop and see if there's a science institute not far from the forest."

"Here?"

"Why not? No one is going to snatch it. Too many people in here."

"It'll draw attention."

"So what?"

Still a bit hesitant, he opened his backpack and took the computer out. Instead of setting it on the table, he put it on the seat next to him, thereby hiding it from prying eyes. "I'm surprised you haven't bought one of these," he said softly.

"I've thought about it, but the idea of lugging it around with me wasn't lucrative. I'm surprised that yours hasn't been stolen. You can't wear your backpack if you have to get out of the patrol car to deal with thugs."

"No, but the vehicle is locked if we're not in it. And we're never far from the car. And yes, there is a science institute not far from the Valley of the Giants. It's called Engineering and Enhancement Science Institute."

"That's where we should start."

"How do you propose we get in there to ask questions? What would we say? Hey, guys, do you create engineered babies? Guess what, we're two of them!"

"Don't be ridiculous. We need to come up with something believable. And when? It's in Oregon, not next door exactly."

"There is still the question of our necklaces. Whoever

placed us in those hollow trees has to be the same person. And this is twenty-five years later. Well, for me. For you, twenty-three. Is that man or woman still there? And there's something off with the chains and pendants... They're magical or something, as we've both discovered."

"There is only one way to find out. We need to go to Oregon. I've got accumulated holidays. What about you?"

He nodded. "Yes, me, too. I haven't taken leave for I don't know how long. But we need to wait until spring. The precinct is short-staffed right now as it is, and I've only just started there. Schmidt would have a fit."

"Yes, and also, if both of us take leave at the same time, that will look suspicious."

"I can go alone."

"No way. We can't go for a while. We'll figure something out."

"Have you got a passport?"

"No. Do you?"

"Yes. I went to New York when I lived in Ontario. Can't get across the border without one. That's first on the list. You need to apply for one. You can apply online on my computer, but you'll have to go to the passport center to get it implanted in your arm. I'll set up an email account for you. Do you have a birth certificate?"

"Yes. Thankfully, Mom looked after all that when she got the job at the Rivera Estate. My SIN is tattooed on my thigh, and my birth certificate on the other thigh. How she managed to do all that is a mystery. Maybe the Riveras helped her with it. And, of course, my driver's license." She tapped her wrist where it was implanted. "Where do they put a passport?"

"Maybe somewhere on one of your arms. They ask where you'd like it. It needs to be in an accessible place to show it to customs. Unless you want to strip?"

Just when they decided to leave, Shep's phone rang. He

answered and listened. "Yes, that's fine. No, I don't want it. Send me the bill, and I'll transfer the funds." He looked at her. "That was about Mom's ashes. They'll get rid of them."

"That's how I did it with my mother's, too. It's just a bunch of dust. I don't believe in keeping them like some people do."

He placed his hands on her shoulders when they got to her door. "I'll see you at four?"

"Yup." She wanted nothing more than to invite him into her room, to crawl into his arms, and have him hold her. But they needed to rest. It was already eleven in the morning, and they had to get up again before four p.m.

He pulled her toward him and held her tight, cupping her head with his large hand. "Sleep tight, my ladylove."

Ladylove...

Abruptly, he let her go and strode to his own room. Arnia opened the door and slipped inside. She took off her clothes and, after wrapping the blanket around her, curled up. She knew she needed to sleep, but it wasn't easy, not after everything they had talked about that morning... All the revelations they had come up with...

Forcing her thoughts into a different direction, focusing on Shep and how she'd heard his heart thumping when he held her, she finally drifted off. But her dreams were not of Shep. They were about laboratories and unborn babies in plastic bubbles...

CHAPTER TWELVE

It was finally spring. The end of March had sent in a warm front that extended into April. She and Shep had spent an exciting few months together as partners…although not so much exciting as very busy. She got to know him really well and couldn't imagine life without him anymore, and in so many more ways than just having him as her partner.

Every now and then, Schmidt hinted at transfers, scaring her. She and Shep tried to hide the chemistry between them, but the captain had picked up on it. Up until now, he still hadn't carried out his threat to separate them. He also begrudgingly admitted several times that they were his best team.

Arnia had fallen in love with the tall, handsome cop. She had broken the vow she had made to herself a long time ago: to never give her heart to a man, to remain single all her life, and to concentrate on trying to make a difference, to make Earth a better place to live in—day by day.

And now here she was…getting ready to go on a three-week camping trip with Shep. Not just camping… They were going to check out the Valley of the Giants and try to figure out the mystery that had boggled their minds these last months.

"We're almost done," said the woman who was inserting Arnia's passport under the skin on her arm just below the shoulder, interrupting Arnia's thoughts.

Another number to memorize. Arnia sighed. Having all that stuff inserted under the skin or tattooed was easier than having to carry it, but a nuisance if your memory wasn't all that great. Thankfully, hers was. She had a photographic memory.

"All done," the woman said after cleaning the area with some alcohol. "Now you can travel."

"Thank you. I'm looking forward to it."

"Lucky you. Where are you going?" the woman asked.

"Camping in Oregon."

"Enjoy. I've heard that it's still beautiful in many areas."

Once upon a time, passports had to be renewed every ten years. Not anymore. Now they were good for a lifetime. And priced accordingly. It took a good chunk of her savings.

She joined Shep, who had waited for her in the waiting room. "All done. Is there anything else they can implant?"

He gave her that endearing grin. "It's a miracle our officer badges aren't implanted."

"Yeah. But they don't last a lifetime. They're only good while we're on the force, and some people don't even last in the service more than the two years they signed up for. I can hardly wait until Monday."

"Don't get your hopes up that we'll solve our mystery. We've got a plan, but it may not be successful."

Arnia nodded. "I know, but besides the main reason we're going to Oregon, it'll be nice to get out of the city. And from what you showed me on your computer, that forest looks and sounds fascinating. And I'm excited about going camping. I've heard that it's fun. I've never been anywhere because doing things alone is no fun. That's why I always preferred not to take my holidays."

"We don't really need to go to the Valley of the Giants, but your wish is my command. It's not like we're going to find the tree where we were found. I doubt our parents left a marker."

Arnia laughed. "You never know. I just want to see where

we came from."

"But I doubt that's where we were born."

"You read the letter. Mom wrote that my skin still had birthing stuff on it, and the cord was wet. That means I was born that day, possibly right there. Maybe you were the same…"

"Who knows? My mother is gone now, so I can't ask her. Now, we're off to buy our camping gear," he said and took her hand as they left the building.

"Did you make a list of everything we'll need?" Arnia asked.

"I did. Not to worry. First on the list is a decent backpack for each of us. Our regular backpacks won't do. Next, we need warm sleeping bags. It's spring, but April can still be cold at night."

"Wouldn't a tent be first on the list?"

"We're just getting a small tent. We don't want to be carrying too much stuff and nothing too heavy. We're going to start by catching a bus to Portland. From there, we'll make our way to Falls City, also by bus. Valley of the Giants is west of Falls City. That's where we'll do most of our hiking."

"You've got it all figured out."

"Yes, the internet is my friend. I've already bought bus tickets, too."

"You're very organized. Have you done much camping?"

"Not for years. I left all that stuff behind when I went to Ontario. And Mom got rid of everything when she sold my grandparents' house."

"Are we going to that science institute first before the forest?"

"It's a privately owned facility and closed to the public. I have no clue yet how we're going to get in there or if it's even possible."

They had to walk quite a long way to the West End to get

to stores that sold camping equipment. There weren't too many stores left, and most people couldn't afford the gear even if they had the time to go on a camping trip.

Arnia let Shep lead her. She didn't have a clue what to buy. The new backpacks were packed to the brim when they left the store. "Are you sure that tent is big enough for two people?" she wondered.

"We only need it for sleeping."

"The backpacks are full already, and we haven't even bought food yet."

"They're not packed properly, silly. We'll pack them the right way when we return to our rooms. We'll pick up the rest of our supplies when we're in Oregon, because we can't take a lot of food across the border anyway. Customs would confiscate most of it."

"And it takes about eight hours to get to Portland?"

"Yes, that's why we're catching the bus that leaves at four in the morning. It gets to Portland around noon. We'll pick up food when we get to Falls City. That bus leaves Portland at two p.m. We'll grab some lunch before we board it."

"I just thought of something. Where will we keep all the stuff we bought when we return? Our rooms will get broken into in no time flat."

He reached with his free arm and gave her a hug. "How would people even know what we've got in our rooms? They can't see through the walls. Anyway, I have a plan."

"And that is?"

"I'll tell you later."

"Damn, this is heavy. I wish we had the cruiser," Arnia complained.

"It's only because you're carrying it awkwardly. It won't feel heavy once it's packed properly and you've got it strapped to your back. And the cruiser wouldn't have done us much good as we're not supposed to take it beyond our patrol route, as you know very well."

"I know," she said and sighed. "Just wishful thinking."

*

Arnia had hardly slept. When Shep knocked on her door at three a.m., she rushed to open it. "I'm ready."

He chuckled. "Excited just a bit? You look very pretty. Different...now that you're not in uniform."

"I hope our uniforms don't get snatched while we're away."

"No one knows we're going away. You didn't tell Dave, did you?"

"No. I thought about it, because sometimes if he doesn't see people for a while, he'll report it to the super, and they'll check to make sure the room wasn't abandoned, or worse...that the person isn't dead."

"Why would anyone want to steal a cop's uniform anyway? Not worth anything on the black market. The boots maybe..."

Arnia took one last glance at herself in the old mirror before putting on her jacket. She'd drawn her hair into a ponytail and put on a little makeup, which she'd splurged on. The jeans felt foreign, and so did the t-shirt. She hadn't worn regular clothing since she became a police officer. Pretty? Hardly... But Shep always complimented her and told her she was beautiful. His compliments stroked her ego and actually caused her to have more confidence in her appearance.

"Let me help you with your backpack," he murmured, placing a kiss on her neck before lifting the pack and helping her strap it on. "Have you got everything?"

"Yup. We should leave the building through the parking garage. That way, no one sees us leaving."

"You're overly paranoid."

"Can't help it. I've lived here more than four years and know what all goes on." She locked her door, felt it to make sure it was secure, before he took her hand, and they began walking to the elevator.

"The bus terminal is on Station Street. Not too far a walk from here."

To her delight, it was an Airbus. The seats were more than comfortable, and they smelled quite new. When it was time to depart, the bus wasn't even half full. Most of the passengers were men, all dressed in business attire.

"We're lucky that they have a bus departing at this time of the night. When I researched it on the internet, they only used to depart beginning at nine a.m., but they added this timeslot for those who have business meetings in the US. And it's an express, only makes one stop," Shep told her after settling in their seats.

"You were able to choose your seats?" she asked.

"Yes, and I got the two front seats. I know you haven't been anywhere, so that'll give you a lovely view of everywhere it drives. The seats recline if you want to have a nap."

"I'm too wound up to sleep."

"You know, I've meant to ask you…why did you move into that building? You said you've lived there for more than four years. Why didn't you stay with your mother after you finished your training and were posted at the precinct?"

"Evelyn Rivera said I had to leave once I graduated from high school. Her two kids went to university. I was sort of a companion for her daughter, and so there was no reason for me to live there any longer."

"But your mother was there."

"That didn't count."

"Must have been quite a challenge moving from a wealthy home to that decrepit building."

"Kind of. Mom and I had a very small room on the Rivera

Estate in the servant quarters. I missed being able to shower more often and the food. Mrs. Rivera insisted I shower every day in the house because I was always with Suzanne, her daughter. She didn't want her to catch anything... I always had my meals in the kitchen with the Rivera kids and had the same food as they did. I quite often snuck food out for my mother. The servants' meals mainly consisted of bread, stew, and soups, all made with the leftovers from their food."

"Still a much better life than living on the streets or in the room you have now."

She shrugged dismissively. "I suppose."

It was still dark, so she couldn't see much yet. Without wanting to, the purring of the engine and movement caused her to doze off anyway.

A slight jerking startled her awake. "Damn, I fell asleep. Where are we? The bus has stopped?"

"Portland. You slept for quite a while."

"Don't let me fall asleep again," she told Shep.

"You needed it. You've been hyped up for days."

"But I want to see and experience everything."

"You can see it on the way back."

CHAPTER THIRTEEN

The bus to Falls City pulled out of the Portland bus station. From what Arnia could see, the city was in just as bad shape as Vancouver. But as they drove on, the surroundings became greener and more picturesque. She saw numerous homeless people trekking along the side of the road, wheeling old rusty shopping carts or falling-apart baby strollers filled with whatever belongings they had scrounged up. Where were they all going? Were they looking for a better place to make their camp?

"We're almost in Falls City," Shep said. "I've booked a room for us in a motel for two nights."

"No camping?"

"We'll do our camping in the Valley of the Giants. Tomorrow, we'll look for the science institute."

She snuggled against him and rested her head on his shoulder. "I'm so glad you're with me in this. You're my shepherd."

That deep chuckle that always sent tremors down her spine. "Your shepherd, huh?"

"Yeah, you guide me, lead me. Isn't that what shepherds do?"

"Eh, they herd sheep and cattle."

"Then I'm your sheep."

"Ha ha, my little lost lamb."

"Not quite a lost lamb."

He kissed the top of her head. "No, far from lost. You're home with me, baby, and I'll never let you stray."

He always knew exactly what to say to make her feel like a million dollars. She was his...for keeps. But sometimes, she still couldn't help feeling uncertain. Not about her own feelings. She loved him. But did he love her just as much? His words indicated he did, but it was still so new, so fresh. And their relationship still hadn't evolved to deeper levels. She was still hesitant to give him her all. Would that drive him away from her eventually? Not that she'd keep him at arm's length forever... Hell, no. She wanted him just as badly. And what about the mystery that surrounded them? Would that tear them apart?

So far, it had brought them much closer together. But was there even the slightest possibility that similar DNA ran through their veins? If they were engineered infants, it was a possibility. A mixture of blood had to run through her veins, resulting in her deep-blue eyes. And her skin wasn't ebony... And neither was her hair jet black. Shep, on the other hand, was pure Germanic or Scandinavian. A Viking warrior... Bright blue eyes, almost platinum hair, and his ivory skin testified to that.

So many different scenarios had played off in her mind, hypotheses that she hadn't shared with Shep. Thoughts that scared her.

"We're here, hon."

"Small town."

"Yes, on the website, it states that it has fewer than a thousand residents now. Not counting the homeless of course."

"I didn't see many of those here."

"Not enough bins for them to scrounge through, I guess. They mainly stick to the bigger cities."

"I saw some on the road."

"So did I. Probably heading to California or one of the other states."

They waited for the driver to unload their backpacks. "There is only one motel left open here. Yesteryear Motel," Shep told her. "We drove past it. I doubt they get many vacationers coming here anymore. The few people that were left on the bus besides us probably live here."

"That river we passed…and the waterfalls. It's gorgeous here."

"Luckiamute Falls. We can do some sightseeing here before we go to the Valley of the Giants. There are more waterfalls here. There are very few places to eat if you're on foot. Like we are. I found one online that's called The Bread Board. It's been around for hundreds of years. They mainly serve bread, pizza, hot dogs, salads, and some sweet stuff, but no burgers or anything to do with meat. I guess we'll go there for dinner."

"Is there a grocery store?"

"According to the internet, there is only one, and it's on Main Street. We'll shop there for our supplies before we go to the forest."

"Where is that science institute?"

"Nestled against the mountain on the other side of the river. It's quite hidden. I found only one picture of it on the web, and it wasn't a clear photo."

They came to The Bread Board. It looked quite neglected, and Arnia wondered if it was even open. But just then, a man came out through the doors.

"Let's go check it out," Shep said.

Inside, it was quite tidy and clean and empty of tables and customers. "Can I help you?" a young woman asked.

"We'd like to order some dinner, but I don't see any tables. Are you still open for business?"

"We only do takeout. You can place your order now or

phone it in. Would you like a menu? Are you just passing through?"

"We're staying at Yesteryear Motel for a few days. We haven't checked in yet."

"Ah, I see. If you'd like to order, we'll deliver." She handed them each a menu.

"Pizza?" Arnia asked.

"Yes, sounds good. And a salad," he said, and handed the menus back to the woman.

"Extra large? Medium? What kind of toppings?"

"Extra large, please, and loaded with everything." Shep paid and gave her his name.

"We'll deliver in about an hour, Mr. Daniels. We'll get your room number from the clerk at the motel."

Arnia waited outside while Shep checked in at the motel. "We're in room six," he told her. "It has two beds. I told the clerk that we are expecting a food delivery. Oh, and I told the woman to make it a loaded pizza, but I didn't even ask you what you like and don't like. We've never eaten pizza together."

"I can't remember the last time I had pizza. I think when I was still living on the Rivera Estate. There are no pizza places anywhere near where we live or even on the patrol route."

"Have you and Scott had the same route all these years?" Shep asked while opening the door to their room.

"Yes, pretty much." A musty smell greeted them. "Yuck, it stinks in here as if it's wet," Arnia commented, pulling up her nose.

"The clerk said they get very few travelers staying here. Most of the rooms are rented out permanently. And I counted at least twelve doors. Let's leave the door open for a while."

Arnia checked out the bathroom and yelped when she saw cockroaches on the shower floor. Shep was beside her in an instant.

"What's wrong?"

She pointed. "We have company."

He chuckled and shrugged. "They'll wash down the drain. Oh, forgot to tell you. Only ten minutes of hot water per day. After that, it's cold water only. I guess we can share."

Share? The cockroaches forgotten for now, she thought about that. *Both of us naked in a shower? That is playing with fire...*

She put her backpack on one of the beds and pulled the cover back of the other one and yelped again. "Oh no!"

"More cockroaches." Shep promptly pulled the bedding off the bed and, walking to the door, held it outside, then shook it all vigorously. "There. That takes care of them."

Arnia stood staring at the mattress. "I don't see any more. What if they come back during the night?"

"Then we have company. They don't bite."

"It almost makes me appreciate my little room at home. At least there are no cockroaches or vermin." She peered at the floor. "Next, we'll have rats scurrying about, or mice."

"That's an idea. We'll leave some food in the pizza box and put it on the floor near the door. That will attract the pests, and they'll leave us alone."

"You're handling it all quite well, as if this is normal."

"We could always leave after we've eaten and set up the tent somewhere, but we've got more than two weeks of sleeping in it, and I'd kind of like a real bed as long as possible. And don't forget, there won't be any showers when we're roughing it. Just a very cold river."

"Better than cockroaches," she grumbled. "I'm going to shower before the pizza gets here." She took her boots and clothes off inside the bathroom and, opening the door slightly, threw them on the bed. She turned on the cold water first and watched the cockroaches wash down the drain, then she turned on the hot water and stepped under the stream.

95

Trying to forget about the dark brown slimy insects, she closed her eyes and began to wash herself using the small bottle of soap provided. But within a minute, she felt movement behind her and a body joining her. Her heart sped up, and fire coursed through her veins when his hands soaped her back. Tenderly, slowly, paying extra attention to her buttocks. Taking a deep breath, she leaned back against his strong chest, and when his hands stole around her and soaped her breasts, she didn't protest.

The possibility of this happening had haunted her ever since they began making plans to take their vacation together and go to Oregon to figure out their mysterious beginnings. Should she let it go on? Give herself to him? She drew in a sharp breath when he played with her nipples, turning them into hard pebbles. His lips were on her neck while his hands wandered further, downward…

Just then, the water cooled and turned icy cold, turning her libido off instantly. She swiveled and looked into his eyes. "Not yet," she said softly and stepped out of his arms and the shower, but not before she'd laid eyes on that magnificent erection.

Arnia heard him turn off the water. She grabbed one of the towels off the rack, wound it around herself, and left the bathroom.

So close…

Shep came out of the bathroom wearing nothing. He didn't say anything and quickly put on his clothes, just in time because the knock on the door indicated that their food had arrived.

CHAPTER FOURTEEN

It was just after five a.m. Arnia was surprised that she slept at all. They'd shared the one bed that appeared to be free of cockroaches after Shep had shaken out the bedding again and remade it.

He was still snoring softly when she woke up. Gingerly, she looked at the bedding but saw no insects. Carefully, she removed his arm from around her, but before stepping onto the floor, she examined the area for cockroaches. There weren't any. As predicted, they had congregated around the large pizza box and almost-empty salad container. She shivered at the sight of the slimy little bastards.

"You're awake," he mumbled behind her.

"Yup. Can't wait to begin our investigation."

"After I'm dressed, I'll go and ask the clerk the best way to get to the institute," he told her while getting out of bed.

"Are you excited?" she asked while pulling on her jeans and t-shirt.

"Not really. I don't expect to get any answers there. That's if we even get to talk to anyone. Which I doubt."

"You're so negative."

"Honey, we're talking over twenty-five years ago. The people working there now might not have been working there then, and might know nothing. That's if we get a chance to ask questions. You need to stay realistic. We may never find out how we ended up in those trees and just remember this as an enjoyable camping trip."

"Preferably without cockroaches."

"Only one more night here. After that, we sleep in a very clean, cockroach-free tent. I don't know what we're going to do about breakfast. We can hardly eat the leftovers," he said with a grimace, pointing at the leftover cockroach-encrusted pizza slices.

"It kept them away from us, at least. If that pizza place is open, maybe we can grab a hot dog there. Do you think it's safe to leave our backpacks in the room?"

"We have no choice. Unless we want to lug them along. I'll be back shortly. I'll go and ask the clerk about getting there."

He wasn't gone for very long. Arnia looked at him expectantly. "And?"

"The clerk told me how to get there, but he wasn't very encouraging. He says it's surrounded by an electric wire fence, is heavily guarded, and they don't allow the public through the gates. I've got no clue how we're going to ask anyone anything."

"All we can do is go there and try. Talk to the guards and see if they'll allow us through."

"How? Do you feel like telling them the reason?"

"Eh...no. It sounds too unbelievable. Babies that were found in hollow trees. They'd laugh at us."

"Yes, especially the guards. We need to be able to talk to one of the scientists."

"It's still early. What about if we hang around the area and try to stop one of the people who work there before they get to the gates?" Arnia suggested.

"How?"

"I could lie on the ground and pretend to be hurt or something. Twisted my ankle?"

"They might just call an ambulance."

"Does this small town even have an ambulance service? Or

a fire department? A sheriff?"

He took his laptop out of the backpack. After searching for a while, he shook his head. "Volunteer firefighters. I don't see anything about a sheriff or ambulance service. This town is so small. The clerk told me that the population here is less than five hundred now. But your idea might be a good one. Maybe they'd take us into the institute while waiting for help."

"There must be some kind of ambulatory service. What if someone has an accident?"

"There might not even be a doctor here. I just found a bigger city not too far from here. Dallas. That's probably where people go to see a doctor or where they call if an ambulance is needed."

"A twisted ankle isn't serious enough for an ambulance. It was just a thought. Let's just go there and see if we can find a way to get through that fence," Arnia suggested.

"It's electric."

"Then I don't know. I wonder where the people who work in the institute live. If any of them live here, we could spy on them and approach them somehow."

He snorted. "Yeah, at one of the many restaurants. Sweetheart, we may have made this trip for nothing."

"Not for nothing. It beats sitting in our small rooms or spending the holiday roaming around Vancouver. I look at it as an adventure."

"You're right. But I should have said that we probably won't get the answers we're looking for. We'll enjoy the camping part of it."

"Let's go and check out the institute anyway."

"If you insist. But we need to find some breakfast first."

After Shep got dressed, he dug up his small backpack and slipped his computer into it. "You ready to go?"

"Yup. Should I take my other backpack, too?"

"Yes, because if we can buy food somewhere, we can stock

up for the day."

They went to the motel's office first, which was already open even though it was only seven a.m. "Morning," Shep greeted the clerk. We're wondering where we can get some breakfast."

The young man, who couldn't be more than eighteen, shrugged. "The only place in town is The Bread Board. They're open from six in the morning until midnight and serve pretty much anything you ask for."

"Thanks. By the way, is it safe to leave our clothing and stuff in our room?"

"Yeah. Almost no homeless people here in town. The odd one comes sailing through but leaves again just as quick. Nothing to be had here."

"Great. We're going to hike for a bit. See you later."

"I hope he's right," Arnia said. "I'd hate for us to come back to our five-star room and find our things gone."

"Uh-huh. That would put a quick end to our adventures."

All The Bread Board had to offer for breakfast was hot dogs and egg dogs. "Well, let's try the egg dogs," Shep said, ordering three for himself and two for Arnia. He also ordered six hot dogs and drinks for them to take along.

The egg dogs consisted of hard-boiled eggs sliced on hot dog buns and a leaf of lettuce. After eating one, Arnia was full.

The hike to the institute took a while because it was all uphill via a dirt road. Towards nine a.m., several cars passed them.

When they got to a large rolling gate, there was a single guard shack next to it, and it looked like only one guard was on duty. The gate was closed. The guard stepped out of the tiny office. "Can I help you?"

Arnia did some quick thinking. "Eh...I'm a student at the Faculty of Science at the University of British Columbia in

Vancouver, commonly known as UBC, and I was wondering if I could speak with some of the scientists here."

"In regard to what?"

"I'm hoping to apprentice."

"Please wait here." He hurried back to his office.

"If someone agrees to talk to you, how are you going to get out of that lie?" Shep wondered softly.

The guard returned. "Due to your unusual request, Doctor Castillo has agreed to see you. I'll open the gate for you. Just walk up to the building and announce your arrival at the office."

"Wow," Shep uttered. "It worked. Now what are you going to tell the good doctor?"

The gate rolled open, and they began the trek up to the building, which was mostly hidden by tall pines. But when they got closer, Arnia noticed that it wasn't just one building but several, all of them one story. They went up wide steps and through glass sliding doors that opened into a large lobby. There was a receptionist seated at a futuristic-looking desk.

"You're here to see Doctor Castillo. Follow me," she told them.

They followed her through a long hallway, at the end of which she knocked on a door. A deep voice answered. "Come in."

Arnia went in first. She faced an elderly man dressed in a white bodysuit and white coat sitting behind a large desk. Glasses perched on his nose, and he was gazing at a floating computer screen. "Take a seat," he finally said, and looked at them. "I'm Doctor Phillip Castillo. Would you like to tell me the truth now?"

"Eh, the-the truth?" Arnia stammered.

"Yes. We don't take apprentices. Your odd request made me suspicious that you're here for a different reason. What are your names? How old are you both?" He ran his fingers through a shock of wild white hair.

"Arnia Powell. I'm twenty-three."

"Shepherd Daniels, twenty-five."

"I see. And you're from Vancouver, British Columbia? Is that true? If I run your names through my extensive database, what am I going to find out about you?"

Arnia made a split decision, to be honest. "Apprenticing was the only excuse I could think of for us to get into the facility to talk to you people. You'll discover that we're cops, but we're here on vacation doing some personal research."

"Research into what?"

His still sharp green eyes bored into Arnia's. She shifted uncomfortably on her chair. "Into our roots."

Her answer caused the doctor to straighten suddenly. He picked up a pencil and tapped it nervously on the desk. "You think you were born in Oregon? You're in the wrong place, my dear, if you're looking for birth records."

Shep spoke up now. "No, I believe we're in exactly the right place. Do you know what this is?" He pulled the chain from beneath his t-shirt, the pendant dangling from his fingers.

Arnia saw the doctor's eyes open wide, his lips tighten, and his face become sickly pale.

"Where did you get that?"

"It was around our necks at birth. Arnia has one, too."

The doctor stood so suddenly that his chair almost tumbled. He reached with shaky hands to steady it. "I see. Come with me." He walked around the desk and held the door open.

Arnia wondered where he was going to take them. The doctor knew something… Of that she was certain. Shep showing him the necklace had shocked him. He led them down another hallway, then another, and finally opened a door.

"Please enter."

She stepped into what she thought was another office, followed by Shep, but then the door slammed behind them, the lock clicked, and they were alone. "Hey! Open the door!" Arnia yelled, yanking the door handle. But the door wouldn't open.

They had been neatly locked inside a small room that only had a simple table and two chairs.

It was like one of the interrogation rooms at the precinct...

CHAPTER FIFTEEN

Arnia sank onto one of the chairs while Shep paced back and forth. "Well, we know now that we're on the right track to get some answers."

Shep stopped and stared at her. "On the right track? We're locked up like a couple of criminals."

"That's telling you something, isn't it? Castillo knows something. You scared the wits out of him when you showed him your pendant."

"I think he was more shocked than scared. We'll just have to wait to see what happens next," he said.

"He's old enough. So he must have been around when we were born. Maybe he's the one who put us in those trees? Or at least knows who did."

"Perhaps." Shep fiddled with the door handle but had to jump back when suddenly the handle turned, and the door opened.

Doctor Castillo came into the room, followed by two guards. "Cuff them," he ordered.

Both guards had weapons. Arnia shook her head at Shep, who looked ready to tackle them.

"Take the guy into the room next door. I want to talk to the young woman alone," the doctor told the guards, who each took Shep by an arm and pushed him out into the hallway.

"Why are you doing this?" Arnia hissed. "All we came here for were possible answers. By detaining us, you're admitting that you had something to do with our birth and abandonment."

He took the chair opposite her and studied her for a few moments. Finally, he asked, "How do you figure that we had anything to do with your birth? This is a research facility, not a hospital or clinic."

"If that's all this is, then why did you lock us in this room? And cuffs? Really? My mother found me in a hollow tree in a forest not far from here. Pretty much the same story for Shep, and since you're the only place around here that remotely resembles a medical clinic…"

"This is a government research facility. We work with highly classified projects."

"And I presume we were one of those classified projects. Am I right?"

"My dear, I don't know *what* you're talking about."

"I am *not* your *dear*. And you very well know what I'm talking about. Twenty-three years ago, you, or one of your associates, abandoned me in a hollow tree in the Valley of the Giants. And two-and-a-half years before that, Shep was abandoned. Also, in a hollow tree. I presume by the same person."

"Interesting story. I'm sure you'll get a lot of attention and followers on social media. Maybe even a book deal."

"There's an idea. I'm sure the media would be interested in our story. Engineering and Enhancement Science Institute? What were Shep and me? Engineered babies? Did you create us in test tubes? How many more of us are there? Did you leave all of them in that forest? And why get rid of us? We didn't measure up to expectations, so you left us in those trees to be eaten by wildlife. How many innocent newborns did you sacrifice this way? But why the necklaces?"

"Your tale will never see the light of day, my dear."

"Oh, really? How will you stop it? Keep us here

indefinitely? Kill us? Our captain knows where we've gone for our holidays. If we don't return, Captain Schmidt will—"

"Will what? Accidents happen to hikers all the time."

Arnia felt a pang of fear. A veiled threat? Would the scientist really go that far? Kill them and make it look like an accident? Had she said too much? "I've left a letter with a friend. If we don't return or if anything strange happens to us, he will send it to the media and a copy to my captain." It wasn't true, but he didn't know that. And now...after saying it, it probably would have been a good idea to leave a letter in her locker...

He ran his fingers through his hair again. Arnia knew she'd made him nervous. Would they really go so far as to get rid of them and have it look accidental?

"How many people have you and your boyfriend told of the circumstances of your birth? Your parents know, your boyfriend's parents. Who else?"

"I want a lawyer. I won't say another word until you arrange legal counsel for both of us."

Would he comply? They weren't criminals under investigation... This was a private facility. She'd thrown the suggestion out there but knew it was futile. There would be no lawyer...

And no one knows where we are...

The doctor scraped his chair back hard along the floor and stood abruptly. "I'll be back. Think carefully about your answers to my questions."

Without a lawyer.

Some of the time, suspects demanded legal representation if they could afford it and were knowledgeable enough. But this man was a scientist, not a cop. And she and Shep weren't really suspects... They hadn't broken the law and were just searching for information about their birth circumstances. Then again, the scientist could lie about them and call the sheriff in Dallas… Make up that they had broken into the place and attacked him or done something illegal…

After a little while, he came back and sat. "I did some research and discovered that you're telling the truth that you're both police officers. Your parents are deceased, and so are those of your partner. Have you thought about my question? How many people have you talked to about your birth details?"

She thought for a moment and decided to be truthful. "No one. The only ones that knew were our parents."

"What does it say on your birth certificate? Show me."

"Eh, it's on my thigh. It says Vancouver is my place of birth. I suppose that's where my mother registered me."

"And the birth date?"

"April twentieth, twenty-six-thirty. That's the day my mother found me."

"You've decided to be honest."

"I haven't lied. I was adopted. My mother found me in a hollow tree in the Valley of the Giants."

"I suppose you haven't got adoption records?"

"No. I didn't even know I was adopted until a few months ago. My mother found me in that tree when she was making her way to Vancouver from California. I was newly born with the umbilical cord still attached. I presume she registered my birth, pretending to have given birth to me herself."

"Doesn't that require a hospital and doctor's name?"

"I don't really know how she registered me. She didn't mention any of that in the letter she left for me."

"And you had the necklace around your neck."

"Apparently. I didn't get that from Mom until a few months ago with the letter explaining everything."

"If I take the cuffs off, will you try anything silly?"

"No. Shep and I don't want to make trouble. We just need answers."

"Why is it so important? Has either of you experienced anything abnormal? Health problems?" he asked while removing the cuffs.

"We're both healthy."

"I see. What made you decide to approach the institute for possible answers?"

"Genetic engineering? We were found on the day of our birth, indicating our birth mothers gave birth in that forest, or we were placed there. I doubt a woman from Falls City would go to the forest to give birth to her child. And there are no hospitals or clinics around..." Arnia kept her gaze steady on the man while she talked. "And there has to be some kind of connection between Shep and me, because we have identical necklaces—exactly the same pendants. Because of that and because we're both foundlings and adopted, we decided to investigate."

He stood suddenly and opened the door. "Bring Officer Daniels in here, please," he ordered one of the guards standing in the hallway.

A sigh of relief escaped Arnia's lips when Shep came in. After Castillo took off the cuffs, Shep stood next to her and laid a hand on her shoulder. "You okay?"

"Yes, I decided to tell Doctor Castillo the truth about why we came here."

"Good, because I did, too."

Because there were only two chairs, Shep remained standing next to Arnia, his hand on her shoulder. It felt comforting.

The door closed, and the scientist gave them each a pointed stare. "I have a feeling you're not telling me everything."

Shep's fingers squeezed her shoulder. The necklaces, the strange way they vibrated and heated up. Had he kept quiet about it, too? Should they talk about it? But she didn't say anything, and neither did Shep.

"Okay, so you're not going to talk. I'm going to tell you something now that's classified. That may loosen your tongue."

Arnia wondered what it could be. Would he finally tell them that they were test tube babies? That he and his associates had abandoned them in the forest?

Doctor Castillo stood, opened the door, and called out to one of the guards. "Bring us three coffees, please."

He sat again. "Oh, I'm sorry. I don't even know if you drink coffee."

"We do," Arnia said. "Coffee would be appreciated."

"Good. Joe will probably be a little while, so I'll begin. About thirty years ago, an alien spaceship crashed not far from here. When—"

"And there was nothing on the news or the internet about it? That's before my time, but you'd think it would be groundbreaking news, and—"

Castillo interrupted Shep. "Let me talk before you draw conclusions. It happened so fast that virtually no one saw the flash of light shooting from the sky. If anyone did, they'd think it was a falling star. Earth's radar systems never picked up on it. My partner and I were outside at the time, enjoying spring weather and having a nightcap. We thought it was a meteor that crashed to Earth. We hurried immediately to the area and found the crashed spaceship. It soon became apparent that we were the only ones who had seen anything."

"The government didn't become involved. That's really weird," Shep mumbled.

"Within moments of our arrival, the ship self-destructed right before our eyes. But two of the crew, a male and a female, survived the crash, though severely wounded. They left the ship just after they had set the self-destruct sequence and found shelter. We found them in the forest in a hollow tree, near death, and brought them here, to the institute. We fought hard to keep them alive, but their physiology was very different from ours, and though we were able to repair their wounds, severe infection set in, and our medicine couldn't help them. They wore translators. Before they died, they told us that they were survivors from a dying planet searching for a world to make their home and that their ship ran into an asteroid and they were separated from their fleet. Their engines were severely damaged, and they crashed here. Besides them, there was a crew of twenty-four and eighty-five of their people. All died in the crash."

"Wow, if the government knew of this, they—"

"They can never know. The couple looked very similar to us, except for their coloring, almost human. The planet they came from was in another galaxy, one we've never heard of. Nor the planet. Its name was Chekondo. The woman was pregnant with twins, and with her last dying breath, she begged us to save her unborn babies, to put the necklaces on them after birth and place them inside the tree for their people to locate and fetch them."

"You *almost* had me thinking that Arnia and I are aliens, but we weren't born until later, and we're certainly not twins," Shep commented. "What does this story have to do with us? How did we end up with the necklaces?"

"Let me get to that. You *are* partially alien."

CHAPTER SIXTEEN

Doctor Castillo might as well have dropped a grenade in the small room. Shep squeezed her shoulder so hard it hurt. "You've got to be kidding," Arnia exclaimed.

There was a knock on the door, and the guard entered carrying a tray with three mugs of coffee and a plate of cookies. He set it on the table. "Will there be anything else, sir?"

"Yes, bring me my laptop, please, and another chair."

The guard came back quite fast. Castillo pulled the chair close to the table for Shep and opened the laptop. When the guard left the room, he arranged it so that they could both see the screen. "What I'm going to show you has not been viewed by anyone except Frank and me."

He opened up a red classified folder, then another, and dozens of pictures showed on the screen.

Arnia gazed at the man and woman lying on hospital beds hooked up to IVs and ventilators. "They are our parents?"

"No, they're not. They told us they were the Originators from a planet called Chekondo. Keep watching."

"They're wearing our necklaces," Shep pointed out.

"Yes, it was their link to their people. A tracker or beacon of some kind. They hoped one of their ships would return to rescue them. Alas, it did not happen," Doctor Castillo said. "From what the woman told me, she was the healer on their ship. That's what she called herself, a healer. I guess she was a doctor."

The pictures and holograms were very clear. When watching the holograms, it was almost as if they were there with the couple. The woman's skin was the same color as Arnia's. She had black hair with a bluish sheen to it, just like Arnia's, but her face was more angular and her eyes somewhat slanted. It was difficult to see the color of her eyes, as she had them closed most of the time. The man had very pale skin and no hair. He was tall and muscular. Except for their coloring, they looked almost human...

"The babies were delivered by a cesarean section. It was a boy and a girl, but they were too premature, and neither drew breath. And the alien woman died not long after."

Castillo paused to drink his coffee, then continued to tell them what happened. "You've obviously heard of test tube babies and genetic engineering. We've been experimenting with that for many years, and it has become quite common now for a well-to-do couple to choose their child's characteristics, coloring, height, and appearance. We extracted a lot of DNA samples from the alien couple and the two infants and began infusing that into the test tube babies we created. Many of them died, unfortunately. The alien DNA appeared to be incompatible. Until we finally had a healthy boy who lived. We did what the alien couple had asked of us, which was to place their own two infants, wearing the necklaces, in the hollow tree where we found them. They had placed a marker inside that tree, a homing signal of some kind for their people to find them. We looked for it but couldn't locate it. Except...their infants didn't make it..."

He stopped to drink some more of his coffee. "The day you drew breath, Shep, we placed one of the necklaces around your neck and brought you to the tree. We posted two guards nearby to keep you safe, to watch for wildlife that could possibly hurt you, and to alert us if they saw anyone approaching the tree. We hoped for contact, to speak to that alien race. That same evening, we went back to the tree to check on you, only to find you gone. The two guards had disappeared. So, we presumed that the homing device had worked, and the aliens had returned, their ship or method of transportation somehow undetected by radar, and taken you with them. And maybe the two guards, too."

"Obviously, I wasn't picked up by aliens," Shep uttered in a sarcastic tone. "But what could have happened to the two guards? Did you ever find out?"

"We didn't look for them, thinking the aliens had taken them. Maybe they ran off feeling uncomfortable with what must have seemed like weird, unethical practices. They had left their lodgings in Falls City and disappeared completely. Secretly, we decided to produce more hybrid babies. But one experiment after another failed, the embryos having an adverse reaction to the alien DNA. Until one baby girl lived. The same as Shep, we took you, Arnia, to the tree, wearing the necklace, and left you inside it. But we had decided to leave you only for a few hours. We didn't want to risk losing more guards. We had installed a camera to record every second and monitor the tree. Except the signal didn't get through to the building. All we got was static. After a few hours or so, Frank and I felt uncomfortable at not being able to monitor you, leaving you there unprotected, so we went back. But you were gone. We searched and found no trace of you or of anyone who could have taken you."

"But you had the camera. It must have shown my mother taking me from the tree, right?" Arnia asked.

"I told you. Static. Blank. It had recorded nothing, so we were none the wiser. We continued the experiments with the alien DNA for a while but met with total failure. None of the test tube babies lived longer than about twelve weeks of gestation. Eventually, we stopped because, after all, we had no idea that if we ever successfully produced more hybrids, the aliens would continue to fetch them. We never discovered anything inside that tree that could be a homing device, a tracker of some kind. We found nothing. So would they continue to return silently to fetch more babies? We didn't want to risk it. Neither did we want to continue to create more test tube babies only to have them die because of their intolerance to the alien DNA infusions."

"But you still play with genetic engineering, right? Most of the science institutes do now. You told me that rich people pay to have you alter their unborn fetus to create the perfect child."

"Yes, something like that. But to put your mind at ease, not too many couples resort to such intervention."

"From what you've just told us, we are humans, but before we drew breath, you altered our DNA, infused us with alien genes. What does that make us?" Arnia asked.

Castillo was quiet for a few moments while he studied them. "To me, you look perfectly human. Your hair has that blue tint to it, Arnia, the same as the alien female, and your eyes are a deep blue, just like hers, and your skin color is the same. The male was naturally bald, as were all their males, the male told us. So, we gave you hair, Shep. Your eyes are just like the alien male's, and you have perfect ivory skin, from what I can see of it, except a tint or two darker. You saw the male in the pictures and the holograms. His skin was much paler, close to very white, almost albino. I wish the two aliens could have told us more, but they were so ill. We fought very hard and tried everything to keep them alive. Alas…we failed."

"Do you remember which hollow tree it was?" Shep asked.

"Yes. We tagged it and have returned regularly, but it's just an ordinary hollow tree."

Arnia let out a long sigh. "None of the trees in that forest are ordinary… What gets me is how no one knew of a crashed spaceship. How did it not show up on Earth's radar? And wouldn't there be a large area in the forest that's destroyed? Bare? Your story doesn't make sense. And if it's true that you altered our DNA, what does that make us? I feel perfectly normal. Hybrids? Is that what we are?"

"Will you allow us to draw blood? To run tests on you?" the scientist asked.

"We've got three weeks' holiday leave, and I sure as hell don't want to spend it being your guinea pig," Shep retorted. "And both of us were tested thoroughly before we became police officers. Nothing abnormal ever showed up in my blood. Or in Arnia's, or she would have known."

"You've got no idea how exciting this is for Frank and me," Castillo informed them. "The aliens never fetched you. Instead, some hikers took you and raised you. If we can test you, test your DNA, your blood, we can find out how much alien DNA is present in your system. I'm not surprised that nothing showed up when you went through the medicals to become officers. They wouldn't have known what to look for. We do. Aren't you curious?"

It was on the tip of Arnia's tongue to tell him about Shep's strength, his X-ray eyes, and her own experience of being able to see a murder in detail after it had already happened and, because of that, identify the killer. But she kept quiet. The man's tale was too much, almost sounding contrived, yet it was also somewhat believable. Because, where did Shep get his powers? From the necklace? From the alien DNA? And she'd had her ability for only a short time. What else could surface in her?

"I think Arnia and I would like to return to our motel. We need to talk, to think about everything you've told us," Shep finally said.

"Remember, you can't tell a soul about anything. Even here, in the institute, Frank and I are the only ones with access to all these files. Where are you staying?"

"Yesteryear Motel in Falls City, but only one more night. After that, we plan to go to the Valley of the Giants to hike and camp there."

"You're staying in that dump? We can offer you accommodation right here. What do you think?"

"Eh...I don't know. Our things are—"

"I can arrange to have your belongings picked up."

"We look forward to camping. Neither Arnia nor I have ever been on a real holiday."

"I'd like to see the hollow tree where our parents found us," Arnia voiced.

"Exactly. And Frank and I can show you where it is. You can still go camping with our guidance. It's dangerous in that forest. There are black bears and cougars, snakes, and more. And the wildlife population has increased considerably over the years, since very few people visit the forest now. I presume you have no weapons?"

"No. We have hunting knives, but that's about it. Can we have some privacy so we can discuss your offer?" Shep asked.

"Yes, I'll take you to the lounge. It's getting near lunch, so maybe you'd like a bite to eat?"

"Where is this Frank?" Arnia asked.

"Oh, sorry. He had to attend a meeting, but I'll introduce him to you shortly after lunch. Come with me."

They followed the scientist out of the room and down the hallway until he opened a door to a pleasant, large room furnished with comfortable chairs and coffee tables. "Here you are. I'll have the guards bring you some lunch. I'll be back in a while with Frank."

Arnia sank into one of the chairs, and Shep took one opposite her. "What do you think?"

Shep's eyebrows lifted. "His story has blown my mind. It's quite fantastic. Do you believe all of it? Do you really think that no one would know that an alien spaceship had crashed here?"

"Not here. In the Valley of the Giants."

"Whatever. Close enough. It would be one of the biggest events in history. I find it very difficult to believe any part of that story."

"We saw the pictures and holograms. That's all real. And what about your super strength? And me being able to see a murder scene?"

Shep snorted. "Those holograms? Manipulation. Look at what they can create for movies. Look at *Avatar*. I don't know if you've ever seen those movies, but the alien characters in them are super realistic. They look almost real."

"Why would they go to all that trouble? For what reason? And according to the doctor, no one but he and the guy named Frank has seen any of it. How many people were working here in those days? Hard to imagine that not one of them talked about a crashed ship or knew of the test tube babies and genetic tampering. Your strength and speed? And how could I have seen that murder exactly as it happened?"

"I'm going to research it on the dark web. If there's any hidden information about a crashed spaceship, it'll be there," Shep said, taking his laptop out of his backpack.

Arnia let her thoughts wander while Shep searched. Castillo's story did sound too fantastical. But what if it were all true? The pictures and holograms looked very real, not doctored. And if it was all true, did she really want to know if she had alien DNA running through her veins?

"I can't find a thing about alien spaceships crashing on Earth. It only comes up with movie titles and books and stuff," Shep told her.

"Maybe it is all true then. Tell me honestly, aren't you

curious to find out if you've got alien DNA swimming around in your body? Think about your super strength. Where does that come from?"

"The necklaces? You know how they vibrate and get hot."

"And how would necklaces cause all that? You got yours when you were sixteen. It took almost ten years for it to surface?"

"Not quite. I finally know now why I excelled in sports in school. I could run faster than anyone, jump farther, higher… Remember, I told you it also surfaced in Ontario in that bar, except I didn't quite connect it all to the necklace. I can't remember if it got warm or vibrated at all. I think it did. I was too busy dealing with the issue."

"All of it is weird. I feel like I'm going to wake up any moment in my room in Vancouver."

The door opened, and a young woman came in carrying a large tray that she placed on a table. "Hi, I'm Gloria, and I've brought you some lunch."

"Thank you."

After Gloria left, Arnia said, "I'm curious how Castillo is explaining us to the rest of the people who work here…"

CHAPTER SEVENTEEN

Their lunch was the best food Arnia had ever eaten. "Do you think they cook their own meals?" she wondered after finally finishing what she'd heaped on her plate.

"Don't know. Presumably, they have a kitchen and a cook. It sure tastes better than any meal I've ever had anywhere. Have you thought about everything? Are we going to allow them to draw blood and do whatever else to test us?"

"Yes, I want to know."

"And then what happens? You do realize they could keep us here indefinitely?"

"As long as we don't tell them about the weird stuff that we experienced, why would they?"

"If they find alien DNA stuff floating around in our bodies... And have you already forgotten that when we first got here, he herded us into that small room and had us cuffed? Come on, Arnia... They're definitely capable of keeping us here if it means they'll get into a heap of trouble themselves for hiding everything they know, for not reporting the crashed spaceship, and because they had the two aliens here."

"Maybe, but if you think clearly, are we going to repeat everything they've told us? Tell people that we've got alien blood flowing through our veins? We'd get thrown into the loony bin so fast we wouldn't have time to think." Arnia fiddled with the leftover food. "It's almost shameful that I can't eat all of this when there are so many hungry souls out there."

He let out a soft grunt. "Right, they'd throw us into the already overfull psychiatric facilities. I think we're a tad too sane for that, my little lamb."

His little lamb… He had begun calling her that after she'd likened him to being her shepherd. And he was, and she needed to listen to him now, follow his guidance, and not be her stubborn self. "All right, I'll go with whatever you decide."

Doctor Castillo returned, followed into the room by a taller, also elderly, man. "Let me introduce my partner. This is Doctor Francois Pelletier. Frank, meet Shepherd Daniels and Arnia Powell."

He shook their hands. "I'm so excited to meet you. Please call me Frank." He sat on one of the chairs. "Phil has filled me in. I do find something puzzling. How did you two find each other?"

"By chance. Arnia has worked at the Vancouver police precinct for four years. I was just recently transferred to it and was assigned as her partner," Shep answered.

"That is sheer coincidence. Also, that you both joined the police force."

Doctor Castillo also took a chair. "It's like fate brought you together."

And had us fall in love… But Arnia didn't say that out loud. "You two will take us to the hollow tree? Today?"

"Yes, after working hours. Have you thought about what I asked?" Doctor Castillo said.

"Doctor Castillo, we don't—" Shep started.

"Please, call me Phil."

"All right. Phil, we don't want to become a pair of guinea pigs to be poked and prodded. How are you going to explain us to the rest of your colleagues here?" Shep demanded to know.

"Like I've already explained, occasionally, we have a couple requesting DNA manipulation of their unborn child, genetic manipulation. You will be such a couple."

"I'm not pregnant," Arnia stated.

"They don't know that. And since I'm the director here, and Frank the assistant director, they won't question us. So, how about it? Will you give us some blood samples? Allow us to run some tests?" Phil asked.

"What kind of tests?"

"Like a complete physical. A brain scan and a full body scan. We'll do it all outside of work hours, and the files will be classified, only accessible to Frank and me."

"What good will it do, if anything?" Arnia asked.

"Just to satisfy our own curious minds," Frank told her. "You've got no idea how excited I am that you are both here and alive and well. But the DNA manipulation must have altered your physiology. Don't you want to find out to what extent?"

"Yes, it'll be interesting to discover how much Chekondo DNA flows through our veins," Shep told them. "But it has to stop there. You do plan to release us, right?"

"Release you? You're not prisoners," Frank told them.

"Your friend here cuffed us," Arnia snapped.

Frank looked at Phil. "You did?"

Phil had the grace to look mortified. "I didn't know what to do."

"Damnit, Phil, we're not monsters."

"Think about it. They know almost everything now."

"Uh-huh. And if they decide to air their tale, who do you think is going to believe them? Remember, there is no proof that an alien ship ever crashed here. There's nothing left on that site. We went over it thoroughly years ago, and that bare spot is quite overgrown now."

Arnia added sarcastically, "And we really wouldn't want to become the government's guinea pigs. *If* they even believed a little of what we'd have to say. All we're interested in is our roots, where we came from. We were test tube babies to begin with. Whose embryos did you use to create us? Or whose eggs and whose sperm? We must have biological parents somewhere."

Phil answered. "We have hundreds of sperm samples and eggs, most of them donated a long time ago. But neither of you would have any resemblance to the original donors. Your DNA was so altered and manipulated that you became your own unique selves. I haven't seen you unclothed, but I suspect that your bodies are perfection."

"Is that what you do when you manipulate DNA for the wealthy? Give them perfect offspring?" Shep wanted to know.

"The few who ask for it are mostly interested in certain alterations, like the husband might have a big nose, and they want their child to have a perfect nose, or infused with certain talent, like musical or art, or the woman is grossly overweight but would like her daughter to have a perfect figure, or perhaps a hereditary health problem that we can eradicate before birth," Frank informed them.

"You two were our own creation—perfection is what we aimed for, besides the added alien DNA," Phil added.

"Because of my coloring, I always believed I was the result of my mother having an affair with an African American man," Arnia told them. "Mom had dark blonde hair and blue eyes."

"And you never asked her?" Frank questioned.

"Yes, but got no answers. I was told to leave it alone. I told you I didn't know I was adopted until recently."

"To change the subject, would you like me to have one of our guards pick up your belongings from the motel?" Phil asked. "That is, presuming you'll stay here for a few days while we run the tests?"

Arnia looked at Shep, who nodded slightly. "Yes, thank you. The room is prepaid until tomorrow, but like you said, it's a dump…with houseguests we prefer not to share with."

"Houseguests?" Frank asked with raised brows.

"Cockroaches."

"Oh my! I'll have you call them to tell them you gave us permission. Do you have the key?" Phil asked.

Shep dug in his backpack and handed Phil the key. "Do you both live here?"

"Frank and I do, yes. When I built the institute forty-two years ago, I had them add a large apartment for a possible custodian. Rather than hire a custodian, my wife and I lived in it until she passed. Frank lived in Falls City. He is a bachelor. After my wife passed away eleven years ago, he moved into the apartment with me."

Phil looked at the time. "Maybe we should get going now. It's about a thirty-mile drive to the Valley of the Giants over bad roads. And then we have to hike to where that tree is."

Frank nodded. "Yes, I'll ask Terry to lock up. We'll be gone a few hours."

"From what you told us, it sounded like it is close to the institute," Arnia said.

"Close enough. But not within walking distance. We'll take the explorer."

Excitement bubbled in Arnia's stomach. They were going to see the place where they'd been found.

They followed the two older men out of the building to a green explorer, a vehicle that could traverse pretty much anything.

"It'll be a bumpy ride," Phil warned them as he started the vehicle and began to drive.

Arnia couldn't get enough of the beautiful scenery. She

was so immersed in nature's beauty they passed that she hardly felt the rocky trip. "It's miraculous," she said softly.

"What is?" Frank asked.

"When you've lived in a broken city all your life, it's hard to imagine there's still beautiful countryside that wasn't destroyed by the aliens when they invaded."

"One day, all evidence of that invasion will be gone, and the world will return to what it once was, will be healed," Frank reassured.

"You think so? That happened in two thousand and eighty-nine, and now it's twenty-six fifty-three. It's already been hundreds of years, and so far, there hasn't been any healing. It has progressively gotten worse. Humanity is on the brink of extinction," Shep commented.

"Maybe it seems like that in the large cities and suburbs, but believe me, give it another couple of hundred years, and that will be behind us," Frank said.

"Not in our lifetime," Arnia concluded.

"No, but as you've seen, there are small towns that weren't severely affected, and there is a lot of beauty left to enjoy."

"Unfortunately, we have to work in order to survive. And work is only available in the cities," Shep answered.

"Unless you can save enough to buy property and become a farmer," Phil said.

"Saving is impossible. A person can barely pay for accommodation and food, let alone put money in the bank," Arnia said sarcastically. "And look at the millions of homeless with no education, no job, just barely surviving on the streets."

"Yes, Frank and I have seen the misery in the cities. And it is worldwide. But we will prevail. All the homeless will eventually disappear. Only the strongest will survive and will rebuild."

Arnia pushed the dismal, futuristic thoughts from her

mind and concentrated on the passing scenery until they stopped.

"From here, we hike," Phil said and got out of the car. "Sundown is around seven-thirty, so we have plenty of time."

While hiking through the forest surrounded by huge tree trunks, Arnia was reminded of her mother's letter and how she'd wished she had a camera. No wonder it was called Valley of the Giants. Looking at the giant tree trunks, it was almost as if she were on an alien planet.

They finally came to a huge tree with a hollow trunk. "This is it," Phil said, pointing at the tree. "The spaceship crashed not too far from here."

Arnia grasped Shep's hand. "This is where we came from," she said softly.

CHAPTER EIGHTEEN

Arnia stared at the tree for a few minutes before she let go of Shep's hand and approached it. "How can you tell that this is the one?" she asked, looking over her shoulder at Phil.

"It is. We've been here often enough, and if you look inside the opening, on the left side is a small metal plaque with our logo on it."

She had to bend a little to go inside the tree. Leaves rustled under her feet, and small dry branches crackled. Suddenly, the necklace began to vibrate and heat. Shep was right behind her. "Do you feel anything?" she whispered, so softly that the two men waiting outside the tree couldn't hear.

"Yes, the necklace. Hear that sound?" he whispered back.

"A soft humming, almost like an angry bee."

"Phil said that the aliens told them there was supposed to be some kind of homing or tracking device inside the tree. Do you see anything?"

"No, but it has to be here somewhere, because our necklaces are reacting strangely. But think about it. Even if the aliens are out there somewhere, it would take them quite a bit of time to get here. Surely, they haven't been quietly orbiting up there in Earth's atmosphere waiting for a signal of some kind?"

Shep snorted. "Thirty more years and without detection? I don't think so."

Arnia saw the small metal plaque fastened just inside the opening. She stepped out of the tree and looked at the waiting scientists. "Can you take us to where the ship crashed?"

"So…did you notice anything spectacular?" Frank asked.

Shep had followed her out. "Nope. Just a hollow tree."

"Exactly. We looked for the supposed homing marker or tracking device, but never found it. We even climbed all the way to the top," Phil said.

But it's there… Arnia knew for sure because of the necklace's reaction. But where, and what did it look like? "I'd love to camp here for a while," she told the two men.

"It's dangerous to camp here," Phil told her. "The number of animals has increased dramatically since tourism discontinued and people stopped hiking through the forest."

"Yet you opted to leave a newborn infant in that tree. Twice," Shep said and let out a disgusted grunt. "And my parents decided to hike through the forest twenty-five years ago. Besides finding me, nothing spectacular happened."

"Yes, they were brave. And so was your mother," Frank said, looking at Arnia.

"Maybe she didn't know about the wild animals. She was told that it was safer to make her way to Vancouver by going through the forests rather than the main roads."

"But why this forest? It's nowhere near British Columbia."

"I've got no idea. She wouldn't have had a map, no sense of direction. Mom was dirt poor. She most probably hiked through here accidentally."

"Well, she ended up finding Vancouver. Quite something for a woman alone with an infant," Frank noted. He looked at Shep. "And how did your parents end up in the Valley of the Giants?"

"They were newlyweds and decided to spend their honeymoon hiking."

"Strange. British Columbia has a lot of beautiful hiking

areas that were untouched by the aliens. Why Oregon?"

"My father was a cop in Dallas. We didn't move to Vancouver, British Columbia, where my mother was from, until Dad died when I was five. To this day, I don't know how and where they met. Mom never told me."

"Ah, that explains it. Dallas isn't that far from City Falls. Let's show you where the ship crashed," Frank told them.

Not too far from the hollow tree was a large round clearing like a giant pockmark amidst the towering trees. The ground was indented by about five feet, even more so in the center. There wasn't a single tree. The area was covered with shrubs and ferns. "In my mind, I can picture a spaceship right there," Arnia said softly. "How did the aliens manage to destroy it so that there was no trace left of it?"

"Alien technology, I guess," Phil answered. "All we found when we got here was bare ground. There was no evidence that a spaceship had ever been here. Not a bit of debris, no charred vegetation... Nothing. If we hadn't discovered the two survivors, we would have thought it a bizarre incident, an unexplained phenomenon."

"And that's why you never reported it? Because there was no evidence?"

"Not of the ship. We did have the two aliens, but we made the decision to keep it quiet until they were healed. As you know, unfortunately, they didn't make it."

"If they had, would you have informed the authorities?" Arnia wondered as they made their way back to the hollow tree.

Phil glanced at her and shook his head. "Since they passed away, it never became an issue. Maybe we would have... Maybe not. I can't really say now after all this time."

"We never came to discussing it," Frank echoed.

"What about the other people working here? Did they all know?" Shep asked.

"No. There is a secret lab just off the apartment. That lab is where we work on our own secret experiments. We had set up a hospital room in it. No one else ever knew what we saw that night or that we had two aliens under our roof, not even my wife."

They had arrived back at the tree. When Arnia leaned against it, her necklace reacted violently. What was it trying to tell her? Was it sending out some kind of signal?

"And what about us? Did the other scientists and employees know of our existence?" Shep pressed for more answers.

"No, because that would have meant revealing our alien visitors and the two preemie babies since we were experimenting with their DNA," Frank answered.

Arnia stepped away from the tree to try to stop the violent reaction of the necklace. "You had someone go and fetch our backpacks from the motel and bring them to the institute. Like we mentioned before, we'd like to spend the night here," Shep said.

"I don't know if —" Phil began hesitantly.

"We'll sleep in the tree," Shep interrupted.

"To what purpose? There are so many cougars and black bears. I think it's too dangerous," Frank told them.

"Because this is where we were placed not long after we drew breath. I want to feel a sense of belonging," Shep said.

"Huh? That's... It's strange you think you would feel...anything," Phil stammered. "You first drew breath in our lab. Not here."

"We came to Oregon to go camping. We'll do so for a few nights before you begin running your tests on us."

"Are you fully prepared for that? Have you bought sufficient supplies? Food?"

"Right... We have all the gear. I forgot we'll need food first. I'm not into hunting for rabbits during the night," Shep answered with a lopsided grin. "I guess we'll need to go shopping first."

"You wouldn't take off on us? You'll still allow us to run some tests?" Phil worried. "If you'll promise that you'll stay, when we go back to fetch your backpacks, we can bring back enough food for a few days."

"How about Arnia and I wait here for you until you come back?" Shep suggested.

The two men walked a little distance away and talked with each other, then returned, and Frank told them, "Okay. I'll go and get your camping gear and food. Phil will wait here with you. We'll also leave our phasers with you. We're not comfortable with you out here at night with no weapons. Although if you don't bother them, the animals should leave you alone. Black bears don't attack easily, and neither do cougars, unless they feel threatened."

"Is there a fire ban yet?" Arnia asked.

"Not yet. You can light up a campfire," Phil told her. "Just promise us you'll call us in a couple of days when you're ready to leave, and we'll come and get you."

*

As promised, Frank returned with their backpacks and several paper bags filled with food just as the sun began to set. "Sorry, we don't go camping, so I don't have a suitable cooler. But you're only staying for a few days. This should be enough food and drinks. It should keep cool inside the tree." He placed the bags inside the tree.

The two men prepared to leave them, but with obvious reluctance. "I've given you our phone numbers, and you've got enough food. No meat, and just in case you feel like hunting for rabbits, don't roast anything at all in the fire. The smell will attract animals," Phil warned. "If you run into any kind of trouble or need something, be sure to call one of us."

"We will. Thank you," Arnia promised.

Not long after the two scientists were gone, night fell. There was a half-moon, but the rays barely filtered through the thick umbrella of pines above them. Earlier, while they waited for Frank, Shep had gathered firewood and kindling. He emptied one of the bags and used it to ignite the kindling. It didn't take long before they had a roaring campfire.

"I can't believe we're doing this," Arnia said. "And we don't even have to set up our tent."

"No, we can sleep in the tree."

"Did your necklace vibrate like crazy?"

"Yes, and I heard that humming sound. It's still vibrating."

The only sound right now was the crackling of the fire. Arnia gazed up at the little bit of night sky they could see. "So many stars. It's a really clear night."

"It is. Do you think the necklaces are sending out some kind of signal? I didn't see anything inside the tree. It's strange how they're reacting so violently when we're close to it or inside it," Shep said and pulled her toward him.

She leaned into his embrace. He felt so safe, so strong. "You weren't serious about feeling some kind of belonging, were you?"

He chuckled. "No... I doubt I'd feel anything of the kind. I wanted to be alone with you for a bit. What they told us today, it's a lot. It's going to take a while to absorb all of it and give it a place in my mind."

"Yes, it sounds so unbelievable. If they knew about your strength, about my ability to solve a murder by the scene completely replaying before my eyes... Hell, they'd be keeping us in that place forever, testing us, experimenting."

"I know. I don't mind them taking some blood and doing a few scans, but that's all. And that should only take a couple of days. After that, we can hike and camp to our heart's content."

"Shep, do you trust them? I mean, what if they lock us up? Want to keep us for a while?"

"They're elderly. I doubt they'll try anything. And don't forget, they've kept a huge secret all these years. If they decided to keep us locked up in the institute, it could cause problems for them, because Schmidt knows we're camping in Oregon, and if we disappear, he'll start an investigation. I told him we were going to the Valley of the Giants," he told her.

"You did?"

"He asked where we were going camping. I didn't see any reason to lie about it."

"You know, I think he suspects that we're more than just partners now. He may decide to break us up, partner us with someone else."

"We'll deal with that when we go back to work. He's short-staffed. I doubt he'll break us up in a hurry."

"I don't know why, but I've got an uncomfortable feeling, as if something isn't right," she said softly. "Do you think it has anything to do with Phil and Frank?"

"I think the two scientists want to run the tests to satisfy their own curiosity. They'll never reveal what happened over thirty years ago."

"I can't help feeling a bit scared."

"Let's see what kind of food Frank brought us and eat something."

The nights were still quite cold. After they had eaten their sandwiches and drank a bottle of water, Shep suggested they crash for the night. "I'll go and get the sleeping bags ready."

"What about the fire?"

"It'll go out. At least it's sending some warmth into the tree and chasing out the dampness," he said.

"Ready," he called out after a few minutes.

When Arnia went into the tree, he had his flashlight on. She noticed he'd zipped their sleeping bags together to make one double. Her heart sped up. She took off her jeans. "Turn your flashlight off."

"Bashful? It's not like I haven't seen it before on Saturday mornings," he said and chuckled.

"That's different."

She quickly took off her t-shirt and crawled in with him. Within seconds, he pulled her into his arms. Her breath caught as her breasts pressed against his chest. He kissed her forehead, then trailed kisses down to her lips. She eagerly waited for him to claim them…

The dim glow of the fire cast flickering shadows into the hollow tree, painting the walls with a primal, almost predatory light. Arnia's breath hitched as Shep's hands slid down her bare back, his fingertips leaving trails of fire that made her skin prickle with anticipation. She trembled, her virgin body a canvas of untouched desire, ready for him.

Shep's lips were on hers, hot and demanding, his tongue slipping past her lips to claim her mouth with a possessive hunger that made her whimper. She could feel his hard cock pressing against her thigh, thick and pulsing, begging for release. The weight of him on top of her was intoxicating, his body a furnace of raw, masculine energy that made her ache in places she hadn't even dared to explore.

"Shep," she gasped, her body trembling with a mix of anticipation and need. "I… I've never…"

"Shh," he murmured, his voice low and hoarse. "I'll take care of you, baby lamb. I'll be gentle, and I'll make it so good for you."

His hands found her breasts, cupping them with a reverence that made her moan. His thumbs brushed over her nipples, teasing them into hard peaks that begged for his mouth. He lowered his head to suck one into his mouth, his tongue swirling around the sensitive bud until she squirmed beneath him, her hips pressing up against his in a wordless plea for more.

"You're so wet," he murmured, his fingers sliding down her stomach to the slick heat between her legs. She gasped as he teased her folds, his fingers brushing over her clit with a feather-light touch that made her cry out. He chuckled darkly, his breath hot against her skin. "You want me, don't you? You want my cock inside that tight little pussy of yours?"

Arnia nodded frantically, her body on fire with need. She didn't care about the dangers of roaming animals, didn't care about the cold night air when he kicked the sleeping bag off, or the crackling fire outside. All she cared about was Shep, about the way he made her feel, about the way his thick, throbbing cock was pressing against her, so close to where she needed him most.

It was time… She'd craved this from almost the first time she'd met him. But now…now she would give herself to him completely. "Please," she begged, her voice breaking. "Please, Shep, I need you."

He didn't make her wait. With a low growl, he positioned himself at her entrance, the tip of his cock pressing against her tight, virginal opening. He pushed in slowly, inch by torturous inch, only pausing for a moment when he came to the barrier. With a gentle push, he broke through and continued to enter her until he was buried to the hilt inside her.

Arnia cried out, her nails digging into his back as she felt herself stretch to accommodate him, the pain mixing with pleasure in a way that made her head spin.

"Fuck," Shep groaned, his voice strained with the effort of holding back. "You're so tight, baby. So fucking tight and I've got no lube." He began to move, his hips rolling against hers in a rhythm that was primal and desperate. Each thrust sent sparks of pleasure racing through her body, her pussy clenching around his cock like a vise. She could feel him everywhere, his body pressed against hers, his breath hot on her skin, his cock filling her so completely it was almost too much. "Easy, baby, easy… This is your first time."

"I don't care! Oh God," she moaned, her hips rising to meet his thrusts. "Shep, I… I think I'm going to…"

"Come for me, baby," he growled, his voice rough with need. "Let me feel your pussy squeeze my cock."

And she did. With a cry of ecstasy, Arnia came apart beneath him, her body shaking with the force of her orgasm. Shep followed shortly after, his cock pulsing inside her as he filled her with his hot, sticky release.

They lay together in the afterglow, their bodies slick with sweat and dripping with the evidence of their passion. Arnia's heart pounded in her chest, her breath coming in ragged gasps as she tried to process what had just happened.

Shep held her close, his arms wrapped around her in a protective embrace. "You okay?" he asked, his voice soft and tender now, a stark contrast to the low growls he'd uttered moments before.

Arnia nodded, a small smile playing on her lips. "Yeah. I'm… It was…perfect."

"Do you know how much I love you?" he whispered near her ear.

"As much as I love you? Do you think our mix of alien DNA has something to do with my intense feelings for you?" she said softly. "I love you so much, it hurts my heart."

He chuckled low in his throat, the sound rumbling through his chest and vibrating against her, sending shivers down her spine.

"I have no idea what that means, but I'll take it as a compliment," he replied playfully. "But we don't need science to explain love, do we? We feel it, and that's all that matters." He gently brushed her hair back from her face, his fingers lingering on her skin. His touch was tender and loving, as if he were caressing an infant.

"I couldn't agree more." She snuggled closer to him, wanting to feel his warmth encasing her like a comforting hug. He rolled onto his back, pulling her on top of him. She rested her head on his chest, listening to the strong, steady beat of his heart. This was where she belonged. With him, in his arms... Her eyelids felt heavy. The emotions of that day finally took their toll, and she slowly drifted off to find her dreams among the stars...

CHAPTER NINETEEN

Arnia's eyelids fluttered open to harsh, unfamiliar light. Her body registered the metal surface beneath her before her mind caught up—unnaturally smooth and chill against her back, yet somehow not quite solid, as if it might dissolve into liquid if she pressed too hard.

She blinked several times, each movement deliberate, testing whether her body still responded to her commands. The ceiling above her wasn't a ceiling at all, but a dome of translucent material that revealed pinpricks of light—stars, she realized with a lurch in her stomach. Not projected stars. Real ones.

Arnia pushed herself upright, her palms slipping slightly on the metal table. A wave of dizziness crashed over her, then receded like a tide pulling back from shore. She pressed her hand to her forehead, finding it damp with cold sweat. Her police training kicked in.

Assess the situation, identify threats, locate exits.

But this wasn't a drug den in East Vancouver or a standoff in Crack Alley. This was something else entirely.

The room around her defied conventional architecture. Walls curved into a ceiling without visible seams, cast in a pale blue-white light that seemed to emanate from everywhere and nowhere at once. Panels of what might have been glass or crystal or something entirely unknown lined the walls, blinking with symbols that resembled no language she'd ever imagined. Some pulsed in patterns that felt almost mathematical, others shifted and flowed like liquid.

A persistent hum vibrated through the table and into her bones—not unpleasant, but alien in its constancy, like the purr of an engine that required no fuel. The air tasted sterile, cleaner than any hospital she'd visited, with an undertone of something faintly sweet that reminded her of ozone after lightning.

Her hand moved instinctively to her throat, finding the familiar contour of her necklace. It felt warmer than usual against her skin, and as her fingers brushed its surface, she felt a subtle pulsing that matched neither her heartbeat nor the room's ambient hum. The sensation sent a chill down her spine that had nothing to do with the temperature.

"Where is Shep?" she whispered.

A seam appeared in the curved wall across from her, spreading noiselessly, forming an archway. Two figures stepped through, moving with a synchronized grace that made them appear to float rather than walk.

Arnia's breath caught in her throat.

The photographs and holograms hadn't prepared her. The male—she assumed it was a male based on what she'd seen—stood at least seven feet tall, with skin so white it seemed to glow from within. His proportions were almost human but subtly wrong. His limbs were longer, joints too fluid, his head slightly larger. He was hairless, his scalp smooth as polished stone. But it was his eyes that froze the blood in her veins, eyes the same color as Shep's, bright translucent cerulean.

The female beside him was much shorter, closer to Arnia's height, and her skin was several shades darker. It was not brown or black, but a deep gray-blue that reminded Arnia of twilight, but maybe the room's lighting caused the color of her skin. Her hair was long and white and moved with an impossible fluidity, as if underwater or in zero gravity. Her eyes were dark blue like Arnia's, and around her neck hung a golden pendant identical to Arnia's own.

She noticed the matching necklace at the male's throat begin to pulse, and Arnia felt her own respond in kind, warming against her skin as if greeting an old friend.

"You are aboard our ship," the male said, his voice neither deep nor high but somehow both at once. His lips moved in perfect sync with the words, yet Arnia couldn't shake the feeling that the sound was arriving in her mind directly, bypassing her ears altogether.

"Who-who- What are you?" Arnia demanded, her voice firmer than she felt. Her fingers gripped the edge of the table until her knuckles whitened. She could feel her police training battling with raw animal fear, each vying for control of her nervous system.

"We are projections of the Originators," the female replied, her voice similar to her companion's but with subtle harmonics that reminded Arnia of wind chimes. "You should know this already."

Arnia swallowed hard. The Originators. The aliens from the crashed ship in the Valley of the Giants, the ones who had provided the DNA that apparently partially made her and Shep…whatever they were. But these couldn't be the same individuals. Those aliens had died decades ago. "The ones who crashed were your ancestors," she told the duo.

The male inclined his head in what might have been acknowledgment. "Ancestors of our line, yes. We share their genetic essence, as you share aspects of ours."

Arnia fought the urge to recoil. Instead, she straightened her spine, shoulders squaring in the posture that had served her through countless interrogations and confrontations. They called themselves projections… But they looked real. "Where is Shep? What have you done with him?"

"Your companion remains in stasis elsewhere on this

vessel," the female stated, her expression unchanging. "He will be awakened when the time is appropriate."

"And when exactly is that?" Arnia demanded, a spark of anger providing welcome heat against the clinical chill of the room.

Neither alien responded immediately. They exchanged a glance that conveyed volumes in its subtle shifts of expression — communication beyond human perception.

"You wish to understand why you are here," the male finally said, not a question but a flat statement of fact.

"That would be a start," Arnia replied, her voice sharp with sarcasm that seemed to bounce off the aliens like water from glass.

The female moved to a panel on the wall, her fingers dancing across symbols that rearranged themselves at her touch. The dome above darkened, and projections appeared in the air between them — double helixes of DNA that rotated slowly, sections highlighting and expanding to reveal complex molecular structures far beyond Arnia's comprehension.

"Your creation was both miracle and necessity," she said, her tone no different than if she were discussing the weather. "Our ancestors faced extinction. Their genetic legacy could not be preserved in pure form. Adaptation was required."

"So we are what... Some kind of science experiment?" The words tasted bitter on Arnia's tongue, though she already knew that was exactly what she and Shep were.

"You are a bridge," the male corrected. "As is your companion. Neither fully human nor fully of our kind. You and your companion are the only successful hybrids of more than thirty years of attempts at integration of several different species from across the universe."

The casual revelation that there had been so many unsuccessful attempts sent ice through Arnia's veins. Phil had already told them about their failures. But how many attempts failed before them? How many newly born infants had not survived the experiments? And how did these aliens know? Were Frank and Phil in communication with them? Across the universe? Were there other worlds out there with life where they had attempted the same experiments?

"It was by chance that one of our ships met with disaster and crashed on Earth, and it was our destiny that our two surviving ancestors were discovered by your two scientists. Without instruction or knowledge, they did exactly what we had been attempting. To merge our DNA successfully with that of a suitable healthy race with the correct DNA in order to synthesize the serum that will heal the remainder of the Chekondo civilization."

"And now you've decided to, what, collect your abandoned DNA investment so you can create some kind of vaccine?" She couldn't keep the edge from her voice. And how the hell did they even know all this? The original two aliens died...

The female tilted her head, the movement slightly too fluid to be human. "You misunderstand. You were never abandoned. You were always monitored by us."

"All these years?" Arnia's voice cracked slightly despite her efforts to remain composed. "You've been watching us our whole lives?"

"We observed. Reported. Protected. Contact was not necessary until it was time."

Arnia's mind raced to Phil's concerned face, his careful explanations about their origins. "And now you've decided it's time for a more...hands-on approach?" she asked, gesturing to the ship around them.

"Events have accelerated beyond predicted parameters," the female said, her voice maintaining its maddening evenness. "The Others have detected your presence. Your genetic signature has become visible to those who wish you harm."

"Others? Genetic signature?" Arnia repeated, cold dread pooling in her stomach. "What others?"

"Those who would see our kind and your kind extinguished entirely," the male replied. "Those who annihilated our world, many of our people, and have hunted us across galaxies to end the existence of our species to the degree where there are only a few of us left. Those in stasis are all that remains of the Chekondo. Earth's people are next, and they have not yet evolved to where they can try to escape the Others. Neither does Earth have the weapons with which to defend their world or the knowledge and ability to stop what is coming."

Arnia's mind struggled to process the implications. Not just aliens—alien factions, alien politics, alien wars, now involving Earth. And somehow, she and Shep had become pawns in a game whose rules she couldn't begin to comprehend.

"I want to see Shep," she said firmly, swinging her legs over the edge of the table. Her bare feet touched the floor, which felt oddly warm and slightly yielding beneath her weight. "Now."

The aliens exchanged another of their inscrutable glances.

"His awakening is scheduled for the next cycle," the female said. "Disrupting the process could cause neural damage."

"Then explain to me exactly what you plan to do with us," Arnia countered, standing fully now.

The male moved to another panel, activating a sequence that caused a portion of the wall to become transparent. Beyond it, Arnia could see the curve of Earth, impossibly blue and fragile against the blackness of space. The sight stole her breath for a moment.

"Protection," he said simply. "And preparation."

"Preparation for what?" Arnia asked, unable to tear her eyes from the view of her home planet, suddenly distant and precious.

"For what comes next," the female replied, as if that explained everything. "The next evolution. The next choice."

Arnia's necklace pulsed more strongly against her skin, almost in protest at the vague answers. She curled her fingers around it, feeling its warmth spread through her arm. "I need more than cryptic statements," she said, turning back to face them. "I'm not going anywhere or doing anything until I see Shep with my own eyes and get some straight answers."

For the first time, something like emotion flickered across the male alien's face — perhaps respect, perhaps amusement, impossible to interpret through the filter of his alien features. But they were merely projections. Were they capable of emotions?

"You exhibit expected traits," he said. "Determination. Protective instincts. Analytical thinking under duress."

"Traits you had the scientists engineer into me?" Arnia asked bitterly.

"Traits that were selected for compatibility," the female corrected. "Your fundamental nature remains human. Enhanced, but human."

Arnia took a deep breath, centering herself. The police officer in her, the one who had talked down armed suspects and navigated hostage situations, took over.

"Here's what's going to happen," she said, her voice steady and authoritative. "You're going to take me to Shep. Then you're going to explain, in detail, what these *Others* are and what threat they pose. And then we're going to discuss options that don't involve kidnapping us from our lives without warning or consent."

The aliens stood motionless, their large eyes unblinking. For a moment, Arnia thought they might refuse, might simply restrain her, or, with their advanced technology, return her to unconsciousness.

Instead, the female made a gesture that might have been acceptance. "Your companion's stasis cycle completes in what you would measure as three hours. You will be permitted to witness his awakening. Until then, information can be provided."

"Start talking," Arnia said, crossing her arms over her chest. She remained standing, unwilling to return to the vulnerable position of lying on the examination table.

As the male began to speak of interstellar conflicts and genetic preservation programs, medicine needed to heal the Chekondo survivors, vaccines, Arnia listened with every cell in her body attuned to the information. Whatever was happening, whatever these beings wanted from her and Shep, she was determined to understand it fully. Knowledge was power, and right now, knowledge was all she could ask for.

The golden necklace pulsed against her skin, a constant reminder of the alien heritage she'd never asked for, now impossible to ignore as she stood among the stars, farther from home than any human had a right to be.

But was she really standing among the stars?

"My…my…n-name…it…is, is…Arnia," she stammered. "This is…is… a dream. I'm still asleep inside the tree in Shep's arms. Next, I'll have a couple of crazy scientists coming into my dream to experiment on me."

CHAPTER TWENTY

Frank sipped his brandy while staring at the flames in the fireplace. "I think we should check on them, Phil. It's been ten days, and they still haven't called. Something could have happened."

Phil nodded somberly. "I doubt it. They didn't have enough food for that many days. My guess is that we spooked them enough that they decided to take off."

"I should have gotten their phone numbers. Then, at least, we could call them. It all happened so unexpectedly and fast. We should go and see if they're okay."

"Now?"

"Why not? It's not that late."

"It's dark."

"That's never stopped us before. Fine, you stay here, but I'm going to the Valley of the Giants." He finished his brandy and set the glass on the side table, then stood.

"Sit. Let's talk for a bit," Phil told him.

"We've talked enough."

"If they're gone, they're gone. What can we do about it? We know where they live, where they work. Let them think about everything they've been told. We can always take a trip to Canada and approach them later," Phil said. "We didn't even know until ten days ago that they're alive and well and living right here on Earth."

Frank picked up the bottle of brandy and refilled his glass, then sank back into his chair. "Tell me, have you ever regretted any of it?"

Phil paused, his hands hovering over the keyboard of his laptop. "Which part? Creating life through unprecedented genetic manipulation? Keeping that creation secret from the world? Using the DNA from two aliens and two human beings as scientific subjects?"

"All of it. Any of it," Frank said, meeting his colleague's gaze.

Phil's eyes, magnified slightly by his glasses, reflected the blue glow of the monitors surrounding them. "I regret the deception. The necessary lies. But them?" He gestured to the holographic displays showing the last images and data of the two infants. "Never. They were...are...extraordinary. The fact that they showed up here blew my mind. Here we thought they'd been whisked into space... All this time, they were alive, living not that far away from us. I wish we had known."

"And then what? Kidnapped them and kept them here?"

"When they return, we need to explain to them how unique they are. How important to humanity's preservation..."

"And tell them exactly why they were created? And what else the alien man divulged to us before he died?"

Frank tapped commands into the holographic interface, and an image materialized in the center of the room—a three-dimensional rendering of the ancient, hollow tree in the Valley of the Giants.

The tree rotated slowly in the air between them, overlaid with colorful data streams that reflected decades of measurements. The scientists had monitored the location since the crash and discovery of the two alien victims, cataloging every fluctuation in the unusual energy signature that had lingered there. Very recently, those fluctuations had intensified, which had surprised them and excited them. But now the fluctuations were explained. The tree had reacted to the two hybrid creations.

"Look at the harmonic resonance pattern," Frank said, isolating one particularly complex data stream.

Phil leaned forward, his skepticism momentarily eclipsed by scientific curiosity. "That could indicate a response loop, not necessarily external contact."

"Then explain this." Frank manipulated the hologram again, highlighting a sudden spike in the data. "This pattern here. It's a perfect match for the carrier wave we detected shortly after the original event."

The original event—their clinical terminology for the spacecraft's crash that had changed everything. Even after thirty years, they avoided discussing it directly, as if naming it might somehow diminish its scientific significance or, perhaps, awaken sleeping ghosts.

Phil studied the data, his forehead creasing into familiar furrows. "It could be equipment malfunction. Solar flare interference. Or—"

"Or exactly what we've been both hoping for and dreading since we first synthesized the alien DNA," Frank interrupted, his voice laced with emotion.

"Contact."

The word hung in the air between them, heavy with implications. The two scientists had dedicated their lives to this project.

And they had waited…

And waited…

"But, if they've been taken—" Phil began again, unable to finish the implication.

"Then maybe they are exactly where they were always meant to be," Frank finished for him, though his tense shoulders betrayed his own uncertainty. "Or…they could be having a friendly cup of tea with alien visitors."

Phil pushed himself up from his chair and moved to a workstation where physical files—actual paper, a rarity in this digital age—were arranged in meticulous chronological order. He pulled out a folder labeled simply 'Contingency' and laid it on the desk. "We need to consider Protocol Omega," he said quietly.

Frank's expression darkened. "Not yet. Not until we're certain."

"And how will we achieve certainty, Frank? Wait another week? What if they're merely in trouble and need our help?" Phil's voice rose slightly, bouncing off the acoustically dampened walls.

"And what if we find them happily drinking tea with the aliens and our interference causes problems?" Phil countered, his hands spreading in frustration. "We are dealing with technology and beings far beyond our understanding. The aliens told us that the pendants were designed as beacons, tracking devices, but also as protection. If contact has occurred and we arrive on the scene, our presence could be seen as…threatening."

Phil's laugh held no humor. "Threatening? Two old scientists with bad knees and failing eyesight?"

"Two scientists who created human-alien hybrids without permission from either species," Frank corrected grimly. "I doubt that would be viewed as a friendly overture."

"But after everything the alien male told us, that integration between their species and humans was necessary to develop a serum to heal their people and a vaccine for us against what's coming?"

"Yes, but he didn't ask us to start playing in their playpen. Their goal was to obtain human DNA and create their own hybrids. Running into that asteroid wasn't part of their plan. Their crash on Earth and contact with us was premature, wasn't planned until much later. We should listen to the recording again. It's been quite a few years since we've listened to it."

Phil frowned. "It's been more than thirty years. The alien might have been wrong with his prediction. And how did he know about the imminent attack on Earth, anyway? He never told us."

"No, he didn't give us a timeframe. But you know very well what he described the germ warfare will do to us." Frank shuddered. "I can't imagine how those beasts were able to develop a disease that will literally melt a body, dissolve it."

Phil's fingers flew over the interface and brought up a recording. "I won't play all of it, just the important part."

A metallic voice echoed through the room. At times, it was just a word or choppy sentences, but the meaning was clear.

"Prepare. The Others… They… You must… We need… Earth in danger. Others… They will kill… It is coming. We… DNA… Your species will not… They attack… We must merge DNA… Antidote… Serum… Warning… Warning… My lifeforce fading… Earth prepare… Cannot stop Others…"

Phil turned it off. "That's enough. Isn't it what he said that prompted us to begin the DNA experiments?"

Frank inclined his head, acknowledging it. "Yes, but it was all so unclear. All that hangs in my head is how we saw the two aliens disintegrate right before our eyes, literally melt like an ice cube in the sun."

"Well, whatever he was all warning us about hasn't happened, and it's been so long now that I doubt it will. And though we were successful in creating two hybrids, how they could be useful against some kind of attack is beyond me. I had really hoped that they would have had extraordinary abilities of some kind, but apparently, that didn't happen. I'm just glad we got to meet them, and they appear to be strong and healthy." Phil brought up the tree again.

The holographic tree continued its slow rotation between them, indifferent to their debate. Data streams flowed through its digital branches, telling a story that neither man fully understood despite decades of study.

"The hollow tree has always been the nexus point," Frank said more gently. "If they've been taken, that's exactly where it happened. We should go, and if they're gone, examine the site, collect fresh data, look for physical evidence."

"And if we find nothing?" Phil asked.

Frank's shoulders drooped slightly. "Then we implement Protocol Omega. But not before. We swore never to tamper with the alien DNA again after the initial trials and the many failures. And now I'm not at all sure that the predicted attack by the so-called Others will ever occur."

"But after the many tests we've run over the years, we're almost sure that we will not meet with more failure. If the aliens have returned and taken Shep and Arnia, we need to create more hybrids to ensure the development of the serum and vaccine needed to combat what is possibly coming."

"Impossible for us since we know nothing about the disease. And how can we be sure that it's finally upon us? Remember that we thought it would come a lot sooner. It's been too many years, Phil."

"Earth was next after the Others annihilated what was left of the Chekondo people. Their timeline is different from ours."

"But it could be that the Others were not successful in obliterating them. Maybe the Chekondo returned to claim two beings they regard as their property."

"They're humans, Frank. Just because we infused them with Chekondo DNA doesn't mean they're the same."

"We're throwing wild guesses out there. We need to simply go and check on them to make sure they're okay. After what we told them, they'll think we were just a couple of old, senile fools. They're probably just having a good time camping."

Phil nodded reluctantly, closing the contingency folder. "We leave at dawn, then. I'll prepare the equipment just in case we need to run tests on the site." He gathered specialized equipment from locked cabinets—devices that looked unremarkable but had been modified to detect energy signatures that standard scientific instruments couldn't perceive. He packed them methodically into shock-resistant cases, each item nested in custom-molded foam.

"I'm worried about them," Frank muttered. For a moment, scientific detachment gave way to something that might have been paternal pride and concern. He had watched them grow from microscopic embryos to newborn infants, and now they were adults with personalities and dreams and fears. Whatever his scientific objectivity demanded, some part of him had never stopped thinking about them as miracles. Miracles who had grown up on Earth, right under their noses, and became two beautiful, perfect human beings…

"They're in danger," Phil said quietly. "I've got a weird gut feeling."

Frank didn't dismiss his colleague's intuition. After thirty years of monitoring unusual genetic expressions and unexplainable phenomena, they had both developed a healthy respect for perceptions that defied scientific explanation.

"Then we will find them," Frank said with a certainty he didn't entirely feel. "Whatever has happened, we will find them."

"Right. The aliens returned after all these years and took them. Let's just quickly put out a call to transport us up to the stars," Phil answered in a sarcastic tone.

The holographic tree flickered as the system automatically refreshed the display, its data streams momentarily disrupted before reforming. In that brief distortion, they both saw something — a pattern, a possibility, a confirmation of their fears.

"Arnia and Shep have either made contact or were abducted… I am almost sure of it," Frank said.

"Dawn," Phil repeated, closing the last equipment case with a definitive click. "Not a minute later."

"And if they're gone? Then what?" Frank asked.

"Then…nothing. All we can do is wait and hope that we see them return."

They continued their preparations in practiced silence. Whatever awaited them at the hollow tree, they would face it armed with decades of shared knowledge.

CHAPTER TWENTY-ONE

Arnia waited impatiently. The two aliens had left her alone in the room. She traced her fingers over the fabric of the robe they had provided for her—a shimmering kaftan that caught the light in delicate silver waves. It clung to her with an uncanny perfection, as though tailored specifically for her body. The sandals they'd provided were equally alien, made of a pliant metallic material that felt weightless yet sturdy. "What is next?" she whispered to herself. Were they going to experiment on her? She thought about horror stories from people who had supposedly been abducted, of what aliens had done to them… If any of them were true. Right now, she wouldn't feel anywhere near at ease until Shep was by her side.

At ease? That was laughable. Her mind replayed what Frank and Phil had told them before all this madness began. Was it possible their warnings had planted some kind of seed in her subconscious? Was this vivid nightmare simply the fruit of that seed? Yet no dream had ever felt this real—the texture of the robe against her skin, the faint hum of machinery in the walls, the peculiar metallic tang in the air. She suddenly noticed the shelf next to the floating examination table. On it stood a strangely shaped object containing liquid. Water? Her throat felt parched…

When the wall opened again, a small figure appeared that she could only describe as a robot. Except it wasn't made of metal, and it wore a bodysuit. It was at least half her size. It was humanoid in basic form but with features that seemed deliberately minimized, eyes without visible irises, its mouth a simple line, no defined nose, just subtle indentations where nostrils would be. Its skin had the same luminescent quality as the male Originator but seemed thinner, almost translucent.

"Follow," it commanded.

Arnia stood, noting the being's movements—designed for function without flourish. "You're taking me to Shep?" For a moment, she thought of overpowering the small being. It wasn't carrying a weapon, not that she could see. But that wouldn't get her anywhere. And how many of them were there on board? *Calm down,* she told herself. *See where the little guy leads you...*

"Follow you where? To Shep?"

The robot did not respond but turned and moved into the corridor. Arnia followed, her training automatically noting details.

Two right turns, one left, a distance of perhaps two hundred meters.

The corridor was wider than she expected. Its metallic surfaces were neither warm nor cool to the occasional brush of her hand against the wall. Recessed lighting created pools of bluish illumination at regular intervals, the shadows between them deep but not impenetrable.

Other small robots like her escort moved through intersecting passageways, none taking notice of the presence of an alien figure aboard the ship. And to them, she must look as alien as they did to her. Some of the robots carried devices she couldn't identify—curved objects that might have been tools or weapons or something with no human equivalent at all. Everything about the environment spoke of function over form, yet there was an undeniable elegance to the design, a sense of purpose that transcended mere utility.

"What are you?" she asked her guide as they walked.

"I am a servitor," it replied without turning. "Designed for specific functions aboard this vessel."

"Designed," Arnia repeated. "You mean you were created?

"Not as you understand the concept."

Its cryptic answers sent shivers down her spine.

They approached a circular wall at the end of the corridor, significantly larger than the others they had passed. It dilated open as they neared, not outward or inward but dilating like an iris, revealing a chamber beyond that glowed with a different quality of light — colder, sharper, with a bluish-white intensity that reminded Arnia of surgical theaters.

"The stasis chamber," her guide announced, then stepped aside to allow her entry.

The room was much bigger than any she'd seen so far, its ceiling vaulting upward at least sixty feet. The walls curved in a perfect circle, lined with what appeared to be pods — dozens of them, arranged in vertical stacks. Most were opaque, their surfaces frosted over, but a few glowed with internal light. The ambient temperature was noticeably lower here, her breath forming small clouds with each exhalation.

A constant hum filled the space, punctuated by occasional hisses and clicks — the sound of advanced machinery maintaining perfect homeostasis for whatever, or whoever, occupied those pods. At the center of the room stood a control console of some kind, its surface covered in flowing symbols similar to those she'd seen on the walls of the first room.

"There," the servitor said, pointing to a horizontal pod near the floor at the far side of the chamber.

Arnia crossed the room, her footsteps echoing slightly on the floor. As she approached the indicated pod, its surface transformed from opaque to transparent, revealing the figure within.

Shep lay suspended in a clear fluid, his eyes closed, his hair floating gently around his face like pale seaweed. He wore a simple, form-fitting bodysuit that mirrored the material of the servitors' clothing. His pendant floated above his chest, occasionally touching him before drifting slightly away again.

"Is he—" she began.

"In suspended animation," the servitor confirmed. "His physical responses to extraction were more severe than yours. This was necessary to stabilize his system."

Arnia placed her hand against the pod's surface. It was neither cold nor warm, existing in some neutral temperature state that seemed to defy basic thermodynamics.

"Can you wake him up?"

The servitor approached the pod and pressed its hand against a previously invisible panel. The symbols on the panel illuminated, flowing beneath its fingers like liquid light.

"Stasis reversal initiated," it announced, handing her a clear container, like the one on the shelf in the room. It contained an orange liquid.

The fluid within the pod began to drain, disappearing into hidden reservoirs. As the liquid level dropped, Shep's body gradually lowered onto a platform at the bottom of the chamber. The last of the fluid vanished, leaving him dry— somehow the transition from suspended in liquid to completely dry occurred without an intermediate wet stage.

A seam appeared on the pod's surface, widening into an opening large enough for Arnia to step through. The servitor stood quietly at a distance.

"Normal consciousness will return within moments," it said. "He must drink the Sjokkum juice. I will return when communication is complete." It retreated to the chamber entrance, taking up a position like a sentinel.

Arnia knelt beside Shep's still form. Up close, she could see the subtle rise and fall of his chest, the occasional movement of his eyes beneath his eyelids. His skin was cool to the touch but warming rapidly. The pendant at his throat seemed to pulse with a subtle light that matched her own—something she'd never noticed before. It appeared to be more than just a beacon or tracker…

His eyelids fluttered open—his eyes, bright cerulean, luminescent in a way that now carried new significance. For a moment, they were unfocused, seeing nothing. Then awareness returned, his gaze sharpening as it found her face.

"Arnia?" His voice was hoarse, as if he'd been shouting, though he'd been unconscious. "Where—" He tried to sit up, his movements uncoordinated.

"Easy," she said, placing a steadying hand on his shoulder. "You're safe. We both are…for now. Here, drink this." She held the strange glass to his lips.

He took a few sips and looked around, taking in the chamber with its rows of pods, the distant servitor, the alien architecture. His hand moved instinctively to his throat, his fingers finding the pendant and gripping it tightly.

"This isn't a dream," he said, the statement halfway between question and realization.

"No," Arnia confirmed. "I thought the same, but I've decided that it's not."

She helped him sit up fully, noting how quickly his coordination returned—faster than would be normal for a human emerging from such deep sedation. Another piece of evidence supporting what they'd been told.

"What do you remember?" she asked.

His brow furrowed. "We were in the tree, and we fell asleep. Then the chain got really hot, and I woke up, but fell asleep again right away." He touched the pendant again. "Then nothing until now." His eyes narrowed as he studied her face. "You know something. I can see it in your eyes."

Arnia nodded, organizing her thoughts with the precision

of a case briefing. "I've been awake longer than you. I've spoken with them briefly—the aliens who brought us here. They call themselves Originators." She gestured at their matching pendants. "These aren't just jewelry, Shep. They're monitoring devices. Tracking chips. Beacons."

His expression remained calm, analytical—the face of a fellow officer evaluating evidence. "What do they want with us?"

"I don't know yet. They speak in riddles. All I know is that we're on their spaceship. Maybe orbiting Earth? I don't know that either."

"Impossible. Earth's radars would detect an alien spaceship orbiting our planet. Man, I'm thirsty." He greedily drank the rest of the juice.

"That's what I thought. But remember, they never detected the spaceship that crashed thirty years ago. Maybe they have cloaking technology."

The servitor glided toward them. "The male's recovery is complete. Follow me."

They climbed out of the pod. Arnia noticed Shep's unsteadiness and grabbed his hand. "I guess we'd better listen to it."

"All of this is blowing my mind," Shep said as they followed the small robot. "I still can't believe any of it. It's a wild dream."

Arnia chuckled. "A wild dream shared by us both?"

"I guess so. Is that even possible?"

"Not in my experience. Then again, I've never been closely connected to anyone."

He squeezed her hand. "You mean we're closely connected?"

"Eh...now in more ways than one," she joked, but inwardly, briefly their night came to mind... Their sweet interlude of love, of becoming one...

Another seamless wall opened to reveal what she could regard as an extremely futuristic sitting room, a room one would only see in a science fiction movie. Two figures sat on a floating coach. "Meet the Originators," she told Shep softly. The male alien stood and held his hand up in greeting.

"Please, join us. You have many questions."

Arnia let go of Shep's hand and gingerly sat on a floating chair, expecting it to give way like a swing. But it remained firmly in place. She noticed Shep had walked up to the alien man, holding out his hand.

"Are you real? Is any of this real?" he asked. But when the male didn't extend his hand, and Shep persisted and reached for the alien's hand, his touch caused a burst of sparks.

"They're not real," Arnia muttered. "They're holograms, projections."

"We are a digital rendition of the species from the planet Chekondo," the apparition told them. "One hundred-twenty-six of Chekondo's inhabitants are in stasis aboard this vessel."

"Why? Where were you going? Or *are* you going?" Shep asked.

"The destination of this vessel was Earth, where our exploration science vessel crashed many years ago."

"And it has taken you this many years to come and investigate the crash?" Shep wanted to know. "Where are the rest of the people from your planet?"

"The only survivors are in stasis aboard this vessel. Like I told you, one hundred-twenty-six. The Others hunted us and one by one destroyed our fleet. This ship is smaller and quite fast. We managed to outrun them and found shelter on a small planet in another galaxy, one that cannot sustain life, but by keeping our people in stasis, we were able to hide from the Others all these years."

Shep snorted. "Sounds like a likely tale. Who are these Others? Aliens? From another planet? And what is the name of the small planet where you hid for so long?"

"We named it Xolosto Six. It is very small, uninhabited, with a harsh climate and bare of any life or vegetation. Since we and the servitors do not need sustenance or oxygen, we were able to mask our presence there until there was no more danger that the Others would find us. We spent all that time learning, evolving, adapting."

Shep snorted again. "You keep calling them Others, but I presume you are referring to aliens from another planet, another world. Does it have a name? Where is it located?"

"Their planet was called Zapusia Seven, and it was located in the Accalarista Star System. Earth's telescopes are not powerful enough to see that far into the universe, and your space travel has not yet developed to where your people could travel to such faraway worlds. The planet was very big, and the Zapusians are monsters, giant insectoid creatures, yet they are quite intelligent. All they know is to kill and destroy. After their own planet met with disaster because of what you call a black hole, they have combed the universe for a new home. Their warship houses over two thousand of their surviving species. If a planet doesn't meet their expectations, they will destroy it. Chekondo was one of those worlds, but we had warning, and more than fifty of our ships were able to escape in time. But not before the Zapusians had already released the killer pathogen into our atmosphere. The escapees became ill and were placed in stasis immediately on all the ships. The Others were furious that so many of us were able to escape, and they have hunted us since. We are all that is left. During their pursuit of us, they continued to attack other worlds. Once they find what they're searching for, their goal is to become masters of the universe. They ignored most of the other planets in your galaxy, as there was nothing of use to them, no inhabitants, no wildlife, no vegetation. Earth has all of that, but they have decided that Earth is not a suitable home for them. It is too small. They are very large creatures."

"Their technology is more advanced than yours?" Arnia asked.

"They kill complete nations, releasing into the atmosphere what you call on Earth, germ warfare, a pathogen they created from a deadly deep-sea creature's excretion. Then, they will plunder a world until there is nothing left and move on to the next planet. And at times, they will destroy a whole planet, like they did Chekondo. Earth is next on their radar."

"And you know this how?" Shep wanted to know.

"The Others may have advanced weapons, but our advanced computer technology is beyond their mental capability. We are able to tap into their systems."

"Spyware. You were able to hack into their database."

"Yes."

"Why have you waited so long to make contact with us? And how was it that the two aliens who died on Earth were real and not holograms like you?" Arnia asked.

"Each of our ships had several hologram projections on board to fly and monitor the vessels. When their vessel was damaged beyond repair, their hologram projections would have awakened them. From what we learned from messages received through our database, there was no time to awaken everyone and evacuate, but without a serum, they would have died anyway, like the two survivors."

"That's why Phil and Frank couldn't heal them when they became so ill," Shep muttered. "When will those Others attack Earth? Do you have a date? Time?"

"Soon."

"And you led them to Earth by contacting us," Arnia stated.

"No, we lost them. During our many years of hiding from them, we evolved technologically. We now have cloaking capability. They can no longer track us, but unfortunately for the Chekondo people, our discovery of the cloaking capability came too late. Now, the Others are in close proximity of Earth because they picked up *your* Chekondo signatures, which has caused them to speed up their planned attack, thinking that they have located us."

"If we try to warn anyone, they won't believe us," Shep said grimly. "You do realize there are still over four billion people left on Earth who survived the alien invasion many years ago. Many of them are already ill and vulnerable. How fast does that virus spread?"

"They will release a powder spray into the atmosphere. Everything that lives and breathes will inhale it. The disease will attack and kill every living human and creature within, according to your timeline, a few weeks."

"How do *we* fit into all this?" Arnia asked.

"We have everything ready to create the antidote, serum, and the vaccine—everything except your DNA, which is a much-needed component. There is no time to give your scientists the formula and list of components, and for them to create it. Also, their level of intellect is not at a point where they could create it without much testing and research. It would take far too long. If you allow us to draw blood from you, we will create the antidote forthwith and will release it into the atmosphere now. It will hopefully protect all living beings and creatures on Earth in time. But just in case some do become ill, by then we will have the serum, and later we'll be able to offer the vaccine as well, if needed. We will infuse the Chekondo who are in stasis with the serum immediately. They will heal while they are still in stasis."

Shep cleared his throat. "And then where will you go after the Chekondo people are healed? Will those Others continue to hunt you? And if they don't succeed in killing everyone on Earth, will they destroy the whole planet? I don't see the purpose in killing people first and then later obliterating an empty world."

"Because they want to take everything from a world that is of use to them. Therefore, they get rid of its inhabitants first."

"I see. And if they see that they haven't destroyed all life on Earth, they'll be super angry. They'll know that something on Earth is protecting humanity," Arnia said.

"Yes, and this will cause a violent physical attack. But we have a plan, which we will initialize as soon as we have assured that all life on Earth is protected."

"Over six hundred years ago, aliens invaded Earth and caused many to die and a lot of destruction. Are the Others those same aliens?" Arnia wondered. "Earth still hasn't recovered from that invasion."

"No, I don't think so, because the Others leave no survivors. And they do not kill physically. They use their germ warfare. And unless we begin immediately to create the antidote to save your people from the Others, it will be too late."

"Then you had better start," Shep said curtly. "But while you're extracting whatever you need from us, tell me how you plan to stop those monsters from destroying Earth completely."

"We will see you in the laboratory shortly."

"And poof, they're gone," Shep mumbled. "Nameless. I never thought to ask them their names."

"Maybe, because they're just holograms and don't have one?" Arnia suggested.

"Since they're projections of two of the real aliens that are in stasis. You'd think they'd have their names. On another note, I wonder how long we've been here and if Frank and Phil know that we're not camping in the tree anymore..."

CHAPTER TWENTY-TWO

Frank looked at the burnt-out campfire and bent to feel the ashes, then he glanced at the abandoned belongings inside the tree. "I think they're gone, Phil, unless they're off hiking somewhere. But I doubt that. They wouldn't have left this garbage, and most of the food would have been eaten by now. And their backpacks are still here."

"Animals have been at the food. Look at the mess. I'm sure the aliens have taken them." Phil held an instrument inside the tree. The needle went haywire, and it beeped loudly. "The readings are off the chart."

Frank looked at the instrument over Phil's shoulder. "Right. But why now, after so many years? It doesn't make sense."

"What if the aliens keep them, and they don't come back? Remember what Arnia said, that she left a letter for the captain of the precinct. Their disappearance could cause quite an investigation."

"When she wrote that letter, she had no clue about us, about anything. I doubt it is true. You worry too much. They will simply be listed as two young people who foolishly went camping in a dangerous area and were possibly attacked by wild animals while hiking. They will be documented as missing, along with the million other unsolved cases. The police in Vancouver have their hands full with everything else that's going on, just like the cops here. Arnia and Shep are not important enough. The Vancouver police are just going to shrug it off."

"True. What worries me more is what the alien male told us on his deathbed. Is this the end of us all? Is the apocalypse upon us? Is that why the aliens took Arnia and Shep?"

"You're really convinced that they've been abducted by them." Frank shook his head. "Phil, you're once again grasping at straws. If the aliens are up there somewhere, how would they even know that Shep and Arnia exist? That we created them? Our two aliens died, and they had no communication devices on them. Remember? And we never did find a beacon or tracker or whatever inside that tree."

"You're probably right. We'd better grab their things. We'll keep them for a while just in case they come back after all."

*

"Follow," the servitor ordered.

Arnia took Shep's hand, and they followed the small robot into the hallway. "Here we go. To the guillotine," Arnia said.

"Don't be silly. They're just going to take some of our blood."

The hologram had called it a small ship, but the hallways seemed endless. How big had their other ships been? Arnia wondered if they were going to be successful in synthesizing the antidote and serum. And if so, where were the Chekondo people going to go? Would they continue their search for a suitable planet, or would they want to remain on Earth?

"You're quiet," Shep said.

"Thinking about everything. Like you said last night, it's a lot to take in. I was wondering where they're going to go after they're healed."

He shrugged. "They've got a fast spaceship and can jump from galaxy to galaxy. There must be suitable planets out there for them. The reason they haven't chosen one, we know... Because of the Others chasing them. But if that threat is gone, they're free to go and live wherever they want."

"There are just over a hundred of them. Is that enough to start again? Build a nation?"

"Maybe they'll want to stay on Earth."

"That's what I was thinking. Earth would benefit from their advanced knowledge, that's for sure."

A round entrance appeared, again like an iris, opening into a large chamber that was, judging by all the equipment, obviously a laboratory. Half a dozen servitors were waiting for them. Arnia wondered if they would be the ones to develop the antidote and serum. But then there was a soft sizzling sound, and the male and female holograms appeared, both dressed in white bodysuits.

"Are you ready?" the female asked.

"We are," Shep answered.

"Please take a seat."

It was like any lab on Earth, except it had a robotic arm that drew their blood—several tubes of it. The waiting servitors took the tubes and went to various workstations.

"How long will it take?" Arnia asked. She didn't hesitate to drink the orange liquid the robot handed to her.

"Not that long. Our methods are far advanced over Earth's."

Arnia wondered how she could know what Earth's methods were, but didn't ask.

"Do you mind if we do a full body scan?" the male asked.

"Go ahead," Arnia said, realizing that they were probably just as curious as Frank and Phil as to how much alien DNA resided in their bodies.

Finally, all the tests seemed to be completed. The male said, "Would you like to eat and drink? I apologize. Since we don't need food, I did not think to ask this before now."

"Yes, that would be nice. But can you now elaborate on what I asked earlier? How are you going to stop those monsters from blowing Earth to a million pieces?"

The hologram's response was immediate, its words brimming with a sense of purpose and urgency. "We will use our cloaking technology and will send false signals to their database to lure the Others away from Earth, and it will lead them on a chase across the galaxy. While they are distracted, we will deploy a beacon on Earth's surface that will emit a signal strong enough to disrupt their ship's navigation systems, causing them to veer completely off course."

Arnia listened intently, her mind racing with the intricacies of the plan unfolding before them. "And how do we ensure that the beacon will work as intended?" she inquired, keeping her voice steady.

The hologram's projection seemed to brighten slightly, a sign of confidence in its response. "The beacon will emit a frequency that specifically targets the technology used by the Others. Once their ships are within range, their systems will be scrambled, rendering them temporarily incapacitated. It will buy us enough time to reprogram their navigation system and lead them away from Earth toward a remote sector of space. We will have reprogrammed their self-destruct command, which will then initiate, and their ship will self-destruct. No one on their ship will be able to override the programming. We will end this once and for all."

Shep nodded, absorbing the details of the plan with a sense of grim determination. Every second counted now, and there was no room for error. "And what about us? How do we fit into this elaborate scheme of yours?" he asked, his tone edged with a hint of skepticism that he obviously struggled to conceal.

The hologram turned its gaze toward Shep, its form shimmering with an otherworldly glow that seemed to pulse with energy. "You will be our contacts on Earth. Based on the information we provide, you will deploy the beacon in a strategic location. Your full cooperation will be invaluable in ensuring the success of this operation." Its words were direct, leaving no room for debate or hesitation.

Arnia felt a surge of adrenaline at the realization that they were being entrusted with such a critical task. The fate of not just themselves but all life on Earth and the surviving Chekondo rested in their hands. She straightened her posture, her voice firm as she spoke. "We understand. We will do whatever it takes."

Shep nodded in agreement. "Give us the coordinates and the necessary tools. We will make sure the beacon is in place before the Others reach Earth's orbit."

"Very well. We will provide you with all the information and equipment you need to carry out this task. Time is of the essence — prepare yourselves. One of the servitors will now direct you to our dining area." The holograms faded, their presence diminishing fast until only a faint shimmer remained in the air.

"How long do you think we were in stasis?" Shep asked while they followed the servitor.

"I've got no idea. It could be hours, could be days. I was damn thirsty when I woke up, and now I'm hungry. If it's days, Frank and Phil will wonder what happened to us."

"I wonder where we'll have to place that beacon."

"Yeah… Just imagine if they want us to place it somewhere like Rome or the Antarctic. They don't realize that we don't have instant transportation, that it could take us days to get the beacon to where it's supposed to go."

"Please enter," the servitor said, interrupting their conversation.

The door closed behind them, and another servitor approached them. "Please be seated." It glided toward something that Arnia supposed was a table and chairs. They appeared to be made of black liquid that looked like it had solidified midair. When she gingerly lowered herself onto the seat, it molded to her body, cradling her comfortably.

Shep sat next to her. He laid a hand on the table. "Interesting. It conforms to the touch."

Another servitor approached carrying a platter. "Greetings, organic guests. I am your culinary interface."

Arnia leaned toward Shep. "Organic?"

He chuckled. "I guess to them we are."

The servitor held out something that resembled a gelatinous tablet. "Tonight's menu has been curated from over four thousand sentient palates across twelve galaxies. Ingestion is optional."

Out of nowhere, floating platters appeared and hovered beside them. The air shimmered with fragrant vapors drifting lazily from them. "I guess we're supposed to choose, except I can't read a word of this," Shep noted.

Arnia turned to the servitor. "I'm sorry. We don't speak this language and can't read the menu. Just serve us."

"As you wish. Your first course is Whimpering Root." It promptly dished up something purple on their plates that curled and uncurled, giving her the shivers.

"I'm not going to touch that," she hissed at Shep. "Just the name gives me the creeps."

"It seems this food is not to your liking," the servitor said, and their plates promptly disappeared, replaced by clean bowls. The servitor placed a square white cube in each bowl and stood back. "This is called Bouche." It sprayed the cubes with a green mist and stepped back.

"Look, the green stuff is liquifying the cubes," Shep said. "It smells like some kind of soup." He picked up a spoon and ladled some into his mouth. Instantly, he spluttered.

"What's wrong?" Arnia said, cautiously returning her

spoon to the bowl.

"My mouth has gone numb. I feel like I'm waiting to get my teeth drilled."

"Wow." She turned to the servitor. "This food is all foreign to us. Do you have bread?"

"I apologize. We have not scanned the culinary preferences on your planet. I will serve the main course. It is called Zarnak Medallions and comes with Broth of Wisdom, Flarnix Petals, and Yuvan Coil."

She looked at the food on the plate. The medallions resembled small steaks, but they moved...neatly rearranging themselves on the plate until a ring of some kind of vegetable surrounded them. "Maybe this is steak?" she whispered.

"I don't know, but it smells good, and I'm really hungry," Shep said, picking up a medallion with his fork and popping it into his mouth. "Not bad at all."

Arnia hesitated, but like Shep, she was hungry. Though the food was strange, the aroma tickled her appetite. She hesitantly tasted one of the round discs and found it quite pleasant. The vegetables weren't that bad either.

When they had finished the main course, the servitor announced dessert. "Scarberry Souffle."

It looked like it was safe to eat. Arnia dug into it. "Yum, tastes like strawberries mixed with cream."

When they were both finished, the servitor handed them each a glass of bubbling liquid that resembled sparkling water.

"It wasn't bad, I guess," Shep commented, "but I'd give anything for a burger with fries right now."

"The Originators await your presence," the servitor announced. "Please extend your limbs so that I may cleanse them."

Arnia giggled when she held out her hands, and the little robot sprayed them with a pink spray that smelled like flowers. Shep received the same treatment.

"Follow," the servitor said.

It didn't guide them back to the room. Instead, they arrived in what looked like a large hangar. The Originators stood beside a small pod barely large enough to hold two people.

"I hope you enjoyed your meal," the male hologram said.

"It was different but good. Thank you," Shep answered.

"The transport is ready. The beacon is on board. We will transport you back to Earth now, where you will place it where directed."

"And where might that be? How far away from home? Or at least from the hollow tree from which you abducted us."

"The coordinates are on this tablet, written in your language," the female hologram told them, handing them what looked like an ordinary iPad. "You are familiar with the area."

"And then what happens?"

"We will initiate the dispersal of the antidote, activate the beacon, and the destruction of the Others will commence. Please board."

A hatch zoomed open. There were two seats inside the round pod. On each seat lay a helmet. "Am I supposed to wear this kaftan? Where are my clothes?" Arnia asked.

The holograms didn't answer. "Please board."

Shrugging her shoulders, Arnia climbed into the pod and picked up the helmet. She watched Shep walk around to the other side and climb in beside her.

For a moment, she felt strange and heard a sizzling sound. When it stopped, the kaftan had disappeared, and she was wearing a silver bodysuit and boots. "Instant glue-on clothes. How convenient."

"Please place the helmets on your heads. They will supply you with the necessary oxygen until you reach Earth. May the universal forces protect you. We will see you soon."

Arnia reached for Shep's hand. He gave her a wan smile and reassuringly squeezed her hand before he placed the helmet over his head. Before she put her helmet on, she said, "And who flies this thing?"

There was no answer. She put on the helmet, and a harness slipped automatically across her shoulders and legs, effectively restraining her tightly against the back of the seat. Shep groped for her hand when a humming sound began, and a slight tremor shook the pod.

CHAPTER TWENTY-THREE

Arnia opened her eyes. For a moment, she had no clue where she was or what was encasing her head. Something also held her body tightly. Memory surfaced… The harness. But just as she fiddled with the tight straps, they loosened automatically.

She lifted the helmet off her head. "It wasn't a dream. This is still real," she muttered and looked beside her at Shep, whose eyes were still closed. She tried to gaze out the viewport, but it was so dirty that she could see nothing. Looking for a handle to open the hatch, she found none. "How the hell do I open this thing?" she muttered.

It suddenly hissed and opened automatically as if it had obeyed her. The fresh scent of pines entered her nostrils, and she gazed out at trees…familiar trees. The pod had landed in a forest, and by the look of the size of the trunks, it was the Valley of the Giants.

It felt like they were on an alien spaceship eating weird food just moments ago, and now here they were…back on Earth. "I don't even remember the pod taking off," she said softly and, turning around, shook Shep's arm. "Wake up, Shep. We're home. I think."

His eyelids fluttered, and finally, he opened his eyes. The harness unlocked, and he sat up. Groping for his helmet, he took it off, then looked at her and beyond her out of the open hatch. "We're back."

"We are. And I don't remember a thing of this little trip. The last thing I recall was getting into the pod and us putting on the helmets." Arnia climbed out. For a moment, her legs felt wobbly, but then she steadied. Shep joined her and put an arm around her waist. "Here we are. And if I'm right, this is the spot where, years ago, that spaceship crashed. We shouldn't be far from the hollow tree." Taking her hand, he pulled her along and into the forest.

There was a sound behind them. Arnia stopped and turned. "Shep, the pod... It's gone. All that's left is the beacon sitting there."

He looked behind. "Just like that. If it weren't for our outfits, I'd still say that none of it was real. I hear voices."

"Yes, so do I. I recognize Phil's voice. What are the odds that they'd be here right now..."

Shep hurried to the center of the circle and retrieved the beacon. It wasn't big, about the size of a baby's head. It was silver, triangular in shape, and looked almost as if it were built from very small silver Lego blocks. He ran back to Arnia and took her hand. "Let's go and see what the scientists are up to."

They sped up, and when they came to the tree, they saw Phil and Frank busy cleaning up a mess, the two backpacks standing nearby. "Phil! Frank!" Shep called out.

The two men shot upright and turned. Phil's mouth hung open, and Frank just stared until he found his voice. "Shep, Arnia, where did you come from? I mean...I didn't hear a thing, and —"

"We have a lot to tell you. How long have we been gone?" Arnia asked.

"Today is the eleventh day since you came to see us. We worried that something had happened to you and decided to investigate. I won't ask where you've been all this time. Your clothing betrays you," Phil said, scanning them from head to toe.

"They took us while we slept, the very first night," Shep told them. "Ten days? Good grief. It didn't seem that long. We've only eaten once."

"Your clothes... And what's that you're carrying?" Frank asked, gazing at the beacon.

"Oh, we have to place that somewhere, and soon. Arnia, what does it say on the tablet?"

She'd almost forgotten about the tablet. She gazed at it now and said, "It's a riddle. I'll read it.

"I never climb, but I descend, My journey has a rushing end. In Oregon's hills, I proudly call, A city named for me — and a fall. Place me on top. Do not let me drop."

"Falls City Falls," Phil told them. "It's a waterfall. And what is the beacon for? Is it a homing device?"

"Kind of. We need to get out of these clothes," Shep said and went to his backpack. "If we show up at the institute wearing these outfits, you can imagine what your employees will think. What time is it?"

"Just after seven a.m. Our people don't start until nine. No one will see you if we leave right now," Frank said.

"We need to get the beacon in place as soon as possible," Arnia reminded him.

"First, I want to hear everything that happened to you both," Phil said.

"No, first the beacon. After that, we can go with you and tell you. It's a lot. I haven't even wrapped my mind around all of it yet," Shep told him. "I'm going to get changed." He had taken his clothes out of the backpack and hurried to the hollow tree.

Arnia took clothing out of her backpack. "So we've been gone ten whole days? Hard to imagine. Like Shep said, we only had one meal..."

"Yes. I guess if they snatched you the first night..." Phil

raised his brows. "How did they? I mean, you must have woken up, and —"

"No, we didn't wake up until we were on their ship. But we'll tell you the whole story later, after we've put the beacon where it's supposed to go." Shep picked up his backpack. "I'm taking this along. I don't think we want to come back here. Do we?" he asked, looking at Arnia.

She vehemently shook her head and lifted her backpack to her shoulders. "Nope."

The scientists drove them to Falls City. After they had parked and gotten out of the car, Phil said, "We'll go with you along the trail, but once we get to the falls, you can continue on your own. Our aging knees aren't into climbing."

The distant sound of rushing water slowly grew into a roar. "Here we are," Phil told them. "You guys can climb up to the top. Be careful. Those rocks up there are slippery."

"Yes, we'd have a hard time fishing you out of the river," Frank echoed.

Arnia and Shep began up the narrow, root-tangled path. The sound of the falls pressed against her ears and filled her chest. The forest around them was dense and damp, thick with cedar, fir, and pine, the trunks wrapped in moss and the branches dripping with mist. Ferns carpeted the ground, and the air smelled of wet stone and living earth.

Finally, they reached the crest, the wide basalt shelf, where the river rushed over the edges, breaking into white water and thunder below. The rocks beneath their boots were now slick and dark, veined green, and glistening. Fine spray dampened their faces.

"This is it," Shep shouted. "I'll take it to the center."

Arnia nodded, her gaze fixed on the wet rocks. "Do it fast and be careful." She held her breath as he made his way to the center of the falls and placed the beacon. A soft pulse of blue light blinked to life beneath his hand.

Activated…

Locked in place…

Ready…

He rose and made his way back to her, his arms out slightly for balance. When he reached the side, he briefly hugged her. "Mission completed. Let's get out of here."

There was only enough room to walk single file. Since tourism had stopped for so many years, the path was overgrown with ferns and covered in wet, slippery leaves.

"Done," Shep told the two men waiting for them.

"Yes, we see the beacon," Phil said loudly to overpower the roar of the falls. "Let's go home."

Home… It sounded good, but home to Arnia was back to Vancouver. She hadn't talked it over with Shep yet. That would come later, but she'd had enough of this camping trip. Their first holiday together would be one they'd never forget… A first… Would the future give them more holidays?

Would they even have a future? Would the beacon do its job and get rid of the Others? Did the aliens release the antidote in time?

The questions roiled through her mind while they drove to the institute.

Once settled in comfortable chairs inside the scientists' apartment, Phil asked, "Are you hungry? I can make you some breakfast, and—"

"We just ate," Shep answered. "Thanks. Coffee would be fantastic."

"There's always coffee." He joined them carrying a tray with four steaming mugs of coffee.

"Now that we're settled comfortably, please begin. Frank and I are eager to hear what all happened, how you were taken, what it was like, and what the aliens did and said."

"Prepare for a long tale," Arnia said. "I'll begin with that it didn't seem that long that we were up there. In all that time, like we already said, we only had one meal. And that meal is a story in itself. Shep, why don't you begin?"

Frank interrupted. "Before you start, that beacon, is it to guide them down here? Are they coming?"

Shep shook his head. "No, it's to save Earth. But let me begin at the beginning."

"Save us?" Phil asked, looking shocked. "From what?"

"Annihilation," Arnia said.

"Fuck! I knew it. The apocalypse!" Frank shouted.

Shep raised his voice. "Please! Let me tell you everything."

Arnia noticed Phil nervously wringing his hands. "Phil, not to worry. Everything is going to be okay. Listen to Shep."

Shep tried again to begin telling them everything from the beginning. "This time, please don't interrupt. That first night, I made a campfire, we ate, and around eight o'clock, we decided to turn in for the night. It was quiet. We didn't see any animals, and we eventually fell asleep. When we woke up, it was on..." he stopped for a moment. "Since Arnia woke up way before me, I'll let her continue for a bit."

Arnia talked for a long time right up to where the servitor took her to Shep, and he was brought out of stasis. "Your turn now," she told him.

Shep continued their tale right up to the pod disappearing and finding Phil and Frank at the hollow tree. "That's it. Everything."

Phil stood and fetched the coffeepot to refill their mugs. When he was done, he sat. Both scientists were quiet, still absorbing everything they'd heard. Finally, Phil spoke. "How will we know if everything happened according to plan?"

Arnia shrugged. "No idea. I suppose if no one on Earth becomes ill...melts."

Frank grunted. "A melting virus. Unbelievable, but now we finally understand what happened when the two aliens died here. They melted while we watched...nothing left of them except a slight stain on the sheet. I hope the Chekondo are able to destroy those bastards!"

"Now you know the purpose of the beacon. And it activated. Did you see it light up?" Shep asked.

"Vaguely. It's small, and we were at the bottom of the falls," Phil said. "I think I saw it change color."

Frank drank some of his coffee, then said, "What I find puzzling is how the Chekondo know everything right from when that spaceship crashed here."

Phil nodded. "Yes, and if all goes well, life here will just continue as if nothing ever happened. We're left with a ton of questions with no answers. And we'll always wonder if they were successful in ridding the universe of those monsters or if they're still out there and will invade us one day. They didn't give you any kind of a communication device?"

"And will they have been successful in creating the serum to heal and save the Chekondo that are in stasis?" Frank wondered.

"That's just one of the many questions to which we'll never have an answer," Phil noted.

"They said we'll be their contacts on Earth. I haven't got a clue how," Shep told them.

"And they never told you where they're going to go once their people are healed?" Frank asked.

"No, they never answered that question. Maybe they want to make their home here?" Arnia suggested.

"If their plan succeeded. For all we know, those monsters might have blown them out of space," Phil said somberly.

"We'll soon find out. If that virus was released in our atmosphere, we'll begin getting reports of people falling ill," Frank pointed out.

"We'll just have to wait and see." Phil looked at Shep and Arnia. "What about you two? Are you going to continue your camping trip? Would you like me to drive you somewhere?"

"I've had my fill of camping for a long time to come," Arnia said. "All I want to do now is go home."

"That's a waste of the rest of your holidays. I'll tell you what, you're both welcome to stay here for the remainder of your vacation. You can go on daily excursions from here," Phil offered. "Right, Frank?"

Frank nodded. "Yes, we have spare rooms."

Arnia looked at Shep, who nodded. "That's very generous of you. I'll gladly accept. Shep?"

"Yes, if you don't mind putting up with us... Sounds great. We'll go shopping and buy food, of course."

"Don't be ridiculous. We'll enjoy cooking for some guests for a change," Phil told them. "At the same time, we can wait out the result of your adventure... See if the apocalypse is soon upon us."

"Or not. If the Chekondo were successful, then that threat is gone forever."

CHAPTER TWENTY-FOUR

There was no epidemic…

No reports of the start of a new, strange virus…

After anxiously waiting for a few days, Arnia, Shep, and the two scientists began to believe that the Chekondo had been successful and that there would be no apocalypse or invasion. Life on Earth would continue as it was….

"I wish we had contact with them of some kind," Arnia said while enjoying her coffee on the sundeck at the back of the scientists' apartment.

"At least we can begin to relax, enjoy the rest of our holiday," Shep answered.

"So the threat of an epidemic is gone, and they must have destroyed the Others, but I wonder if they were successful in developing the serum to heal the Chekondo."

"Yes, and I've thought about all of that, and I still wonder why our blood was necessary to create it. What's in our DNA that was so important for it?" Shep said.

"That's a question even Frank and I don't know the answer to," Phil said while sidling up to them and cradling his coffee, sinking onto one of the lawn chairs.

"Or how they were even aware of our existence…" Arnia mused.

"I've been thinking about that. They look so close to human that they could easily have been moving among us without getting noticed," Phil suggested. "How do we know what the rest of the Chekondo look like? Their coloring? The two who died here… The woman had the same color hair as yours, Arnia. And the man was bald, but otherwise his physical appearance and features were close to ours."

"From what we saw on the holograms, he was very pale-skinned," Shep pointed out.

"But she wasn't. Her coloring was very similar to mine," Arnia reminded them.

Phil sighed. "Too many unanswered questions. But from what you told me, you only ever interacted with their holographic counterparts, not with the actual Chekondo. They were all ill. To answer my own hypothesis, they were in stasis. I doubt the holographic beings would have come to Earth."

"We'll never know now. Their technology was so advanced, maybe they were able to spy on us without physically coming to Earth," Shep said. "That's the only answer."

"Instead of just hanging around Falls City and surroundings, you can use one of our cars to go and do some sightseeing. We're not that far from the ocean. About forty miles," Phil offered.

"Really? You'd trust us with your car?" Arnia asked.

"Definitely. It gathers dust most of the time anyway. Frank and I never go anywhere."

"I don't know what to say," Shep said.

"Nothing. We're enjoying having you visit with us. Neither Frank nor I ever had children. Having you two under our roof is an enjoyable experience. We created you, watched you develop, were with you when you drew your first breath, cut your cords…You're almost like our own."

Arnia noticed that Phil's eyes were suspiciously moist. "I guess you can consider us family then," she told him softly. "We'll come back to visit you and Frank. I promise."

"You're welcome any time. Your rooms will be waiting for you. I guess I'd better get back to work," Phil said abruptly.

After he was gone, Shep said, "That was kind of emotional. He considers himself sort of our father."

"Well, he created us. It's understandable in a way. You don't mind that I promised we'll come back to visit?"

"Nope. How about I go and ask him for the keys to the car? We can go and do some exploring. What do you think of going to the beach tomorrow?"

*

Arnia felt increasingly depressed at the thought of having to return to her small room…to a broken city. After having spent the rest of their vacation in a luxurious apartment, enjoying home-cooked gourmet meals, showering every day with no limit on water—and because the institute had their own generators, there was no limit on hot water either—and enjoying the beautiful countryside, the thought of their dismal existence in Vancouver was a gray cloud that became darker by the day.

"Four more days," Shep reminded her as they sat on a beach looking out over the ocean.

"I love the sea," Arnia said. "What a difference from the ocean back home. Look how blue the water is."

"If only it weren't so cold," Shep complained.

"Phil told me that the water is even cold in summer. Next holiday, if possible, I'd like for us to go further south, to California, or maybe even to Texas. I'm going in for another dip."

Arnia was careful not to go too far. This was her first time ever to experience swimming in the ocean. The water was far too polluted in Vancouver. She loved it, the tangy air, the salt water, the waves… She floated for a bit, trying not to think about their coming departure. Instead, she thought about the first leg of their holidays… The aliens. Did any of that really happen? It just seemed like a faraway dream now. Even the beacon had disappeared. Shep had gone back to the falls with Phil, but the small pyramid was gone. Maybe the aliens had fetched it…or it had fallen, and the rapids had washed it down the river.

The only drawback of their stay with Frank and Phil was that they had separate bedrooms. The two men were rather old-fashioned. They weren't married, so they were given their own rooms.

She was getting too cold, so she left the water and went back to the beach, where she quickly dried off.

"What do you want to do tomorrow? Our last day?" Shep asked when she sat next to him on the warm sand.

"I don't know. I hate the thought of having to go back. But I do love my job."

"You know, there are smaller communities in British Columbia with police stations. Remember I said that I had a plan? We could apply for a transfer to one of them. Choose a small town somewhere."

"Most of those only have one or two cops. Some of them don't have any law enforcement."

"True. But we can look into it. BC is beautiful, too, you know."

"From pictures I've seen, yes, I know. And it could separate us." As she voiced it, a dart of pain shot through her heart.

"After our holidays, I have a gut feeling that Schmidt is going to give us different partners anyway."

"Yes, I know," she said somberly. "Nothing we can do about it. After all this, the thought of going back to my small room—"

"Do you mind if I sit here?" a voice interrupted her.

Irritated, Arnia looked at the voice's owner. It was a

woman in her mid-thirties with long brown hair and unusual golden eyes — eyes that almost seemed to glow. She was about to snap that the beach was almost empty, to go and sit elsewhere, when she spotted the necklace shimmering against the material of a blue floral kaftan. A kaftan similar to the one she'd worn on the alien ship, except for the colors…

It couldn't be…

Could it?

Arnia shifted back until she leaned against Shep. "Shep, do you —"

"Yes." He whispered near her ear, "Another of Phil and Frank's creations? Could she be?"

Arnia shook her head, turned to him, and whispered back, "No. They said they only created two. Us. She's wearing a kaftan just like I had on the ship. My necklace is hot…"

"From the sun."

Arnia turned back to the woman. "Who are you? Where did you get that necklace?"

"I am Zenthia Yllastina Faro, queen of the Chekondo."

Arnia took a moment to absorb what she'd just heard. It was impossible that anyone on Earth besides her, Shep, and the scientists knew of the Chekondo. She sat forward, turned to look at Shep. "Did you hear?"

"I'm not deaf. But how? I mean, is it true? You're from the ship?"

The woman's full, sensual lips formed a wide smile. "Do not look so shocked. Your DNA healed us. I am here to thank you. We are indebted to you both."

Arnia studied the woman closer now. Except for her unusual golden eyes, she could pass for any beautiful woman on Earth. She had an identical necklace…and knew of the Chekondo. This was real. Unless the sun had addled both their brains…

Neither she nor Shep had heard or noticed the woman

approach. She was just suddenly there... "How did you get here?"

"Our technology is far—"

"Advanced, we know," Shep said. "But we were sent back to Earth in a small pod. How did you get here?"

"That technology will take too long to explain. I would like to meet your creators to thank them. Is that possible?"

Arnia looked at Shep. "She's real," she whispered. "They've come to Earth."

Shep nodded. "Yes, we can take you to meet Phil and Frank. Give us a moment to pack our things."

They led the way to the car, the woman following them closely. While they walked, Arnia said softly, "This is going to blow the guys' minds."

"I don't know about theirs. It's blown mine."

"And mine. I wonder if they're all on Earth, somewhere in the vicinity."

Shep turned the aircar on high speed. While returning to the institute, Arnia asked, "Are all the Chekondo healed now?"

"Yes, we are, thanks to the donation of your DNA."

"And the Others—"

"Destroyed. As planned."

"That's a relief. What are your plans now? Where will you go?"

"That is one of the reasons, besides thanking them, I wish to meet with your creators. We like Earth. It is beautiful and compatible with what Chekondo was."

"Are you telling me you would like to settle on Earth?" Arnia asked, shocked. Did the woman realize what kind of commotion it would cause if more than a hundred aliens requested to settle on Earth? One hundred twenty-six, the two projections had told her.

"If this is possible, yes. We have been in stasis for too long and want to settle and go on with our lives."

"Not all of Earth is this beautiful. More than six hundred years ago, we were invaded by an alien species. They destroyed many cities and killed millions. To this day, Earth has not recovered."

"Yes, I know of Earth's history. That particular species will never pose a threat again because the Others destroyed them and their world. But nevertheless, there is much beauty left here, and Earth will heal."

"We are here," Shep announced.

CHAPTER TWENTY-FIVE

It was still afternoon, and Frank and Phil were not in the apartment. "I'll go and fetch them," Shep said.

Arnia pointed at a chair. "Please, take a seat, Zenthia."

Shep returned fast, followed by the two scientists, who looked somewhat flustered. Arnia gathered from their expressions that Shep had quickly told them who was here.

Phil approached the woman and held out his hand. "I am Doctor Phillip Castillo. Welcome to Earth."

She stood, and instead of taking his hand, she merely held hers over his hand, then held it beneath for a moment. "I am Queen Zenthia Yllastina Faro of the Chekondo."

"And I'm Doctor Francois Pelletier," Frank said, but he remained where he was. "People call me Frank."

Phil sank into one of the chairs. "Would you like something to drink? Wine perhaps?"

"Not yet, but thank you. Shep has told you why I am here?"

"Very briefly. Please explain."

"You already know that we were in stasis for a very long time while our two projections operated our ship. When we awoke, we were shocked to learn that the Others had annihilated our fleet. We were fortunate that the two projections found a small planet to hide on for a long time, but due to having to keep our engines running for the stasis chambers, our fuel has almost run out, and our engines need repairs. We cannot obtain this fuel, certain crystals, anywhere except on a certain planet that if it was not destroyed by the Others, is unreachable for us now, and neither can we repair the engines without the necessary components that were only obtainable on Chekondo."

"And Chekondo has been destroyed," Shep interrupted.

"Yes. We need to find a home for my people. Earth is the only planet in this galaxy with a compatible atmosphere."

"You want to come and live here," Frank stated.

"Yes. But I should talk to your leaders, king, or queen, about this, request their permission for us to settle on Earth. Can you arrange that?"

Arnia noticed Frank and Phil look at each other, their faces didn't register the shock they must be feeling. She wondered how they would react to such a request.

After a minute or so, Phil stood, went to the liquor cabinet, took out a bottle of Scotch, and poured himself a stiff drink. He looked around at Frank, who nodded.

"Queen...eh...Zenthia, would you care for some wine now?" Phil asked again. "How about you two?" he asked Shep and Arnia.

Arnia nodded. "Yes, please."

"A beer would be nice," Shep told him.

Arnia finally sat down on one of the dining chairs. When Phil handed her a glass of wine, she sipped it gratefully. She slowly felt it settle the turmoil in her mind and stomach.

"How much longer will your engines last?" Phil asked suddenly. "Maybe we have alternative components to fix them?"

"No, you don't. We can no longer jump to another galaxy. And the engines will last maybe a year to two years. After that, we would aimlessly be adrift in outer space, and we would all die due to lack of oxygen and nutrients. The stasis pods can no longer be operational. They take too much power. And, having to feed over a hundred, we will soon run out of nutrients."

Frank began with a warning. "You asked us to contact our leaders, king, or queen. Earth has many. It is divided into one hundred ninety-five countries, each with its own governing bodies. This country is the United States of America, which has a president who is the head of the government. Were we to contact the authorities that an alien ship requests landing and its occupants are asking to make their home here, it would cause an uproar. And not just here, but across the whole world."

Phil took over. "Yes, more than an uproar. People on Earth have waited for centuries for alien contact. But we know already what will happen. This would be the biggest moment in human history for science. Many people will be captivated. News and social media will explode with theories, memes, and live coverage. Some will see it as a moment of cosmic unity. Others will panic or question your intentions. Everyone will wonder, what are you exactly? Ambassadors? Scouts? Theories will swirl from peaceful coexistence to apocalyptic warnings. You will see both candlelight vigils of welcome and marches demanding answers or rejection. Questions like, can they contribute to society? Will they be allowed to interbreed? I foresee rebellion and mayhem, and you could even be in danger of extremists trying to get rid of you."

Shep added his opinion. "You will never have a moment's peace throughout your lives."

Arnia saw the crestfallen expression on Zenthia's face, and she felt sorry for the woman. "There must be a solution other than getting the authorities involved. They face certain death if they remain in outer space on a dying ship."

Phil ran his fingers through his hair, a habit when he felt frustrated. "I've got a plan forming in my mind. But I need time to put it all together. Frank, come with me to my study, and let's talk. Shep and Arnia, please keep our guest company and entertained. We'll be back in a bit."

*

They were gone for little more than an hour. Before he took his chair again, Phil refilled everyone's glasses and handed Shep another beer. "Frank and I have come up with what we think is a solution. But it will need a lot of cooperation on both sides."

"Yes, anything," Zenthia said.

"First of all, no one on Earth should know of your arrival. You look enough like us Earthlings to pass as such. I have a question. Are there doctors among your people?" Phil asked.

"Yes, two healers."

"Builders? People who can build a home?"

"There are a variety of tradesmen among the survivors. Yes."

"For now, it's just a rough plan, but here it is. I own seven hundred fifty acres not far from Falls City. The land is rough wilderness. It will take a lot of work and machinery to make it habitable. Land needs to be cleared. It will be a tremendous project. There is more than enough room to build a small town. But before we can start with any of it, I have to apply for development and building permits. It'll take a lot, but I think it can all be done."

"Wow," Shep uttered. "That'll be quite an undertaking."

"Yes, and I'll need both of your help to make it happen."

"We have jobs to go back to, and—" Arnia began.

"You'll need to give up your jobs. You'll have new jobs once the town has been constructed and the Chekondo take up residence."

He redirected his conversation back to Zenthia. "We will also have to get all your people new identities. Birth certificates, SSN, etcetera. We can get all of that done on the

191

black market. To begin, we need an area of land cleared up and a large hangar built, big enough to hide your ship. That in itself will take some months. Once the ship is inside the hangar, you can live in it while building the town. Your tradesmen will need to study Earth's building methods, plans, and more. We can provide all the necessary material for them to study while you wait for the hangar to be completed."

"And, of course, all your people will need to learn to speak fluent English. Wear our style of clothing… It is going to take hours and hours of planning," Frank added.

"More than hours. This is just a rough idea of what is going through my mind. We need to talk it through, thoroughly, and all the Chekondo need to be prepared," Phil said.

"And it's going to cost millions," Shep concluded. "Who is going to pay for it all? Having the land helps, but building a whole town… They all need clothing, food, and building materials, and electricity has to be brought in, roads built, just naming a couple of things off the top of my head."

"And how are you going to explain building a whole town to anyone who questions what you're doing?" Arnia wondered.

Phil shrugged. "As I said, this is just preliminary talk. I know we can make it happen." He looked at Zenthia. "What do you think? Is this something you might like? Would you be able to cooperate with us if you agree? You must understand, you could no longer be a queen. Maybe among your people, but there can be no known queen here in the USA. You would become just the leader of your people, what we would call the mayor of the town. And what would your people think of this plan? Would they prefer to take their chances and continue to search for a suitable uninhabited world?"

"There is none in this galaxy," Zenthia said decisively. "Let us discuss your plan in more detail, and I will return to my ship and talk about it with the council members. My ship was disguised as a freighter, but is really the royal transport. It has the royal treasure on board and several of the council. When we fled, we separated the royal household among the fleet. My mate, King Xofornox, and my son, Prince Trumon, were on another ship. Each of my three daughters, the princesses, and the other council members were spread out among the other ships. We did this in fear of attack and to ensure the survival of a royal heir or heiress." She stopped for a moment.

Arnia noticed her eyes pooling. The queen had lost her whole family. "I'm so sorry," she told Zenthia softly.

"Does gold have value on Earth?" Zenthia asked.

"Yes. A lot of value. Why?" Phil asked.

"We can pay for the materials to construct dwellings and whatever is necessary. I will give you all the gold you need. But first, I need to return and talk to my council and my people. The final decision is mine, but I will not make that decision without the full support of my subjects."

"Let us know fast. If you agree, we must immediately begin planning," Phil told her.

"I will return to my ship now." Zenthia stood and walked to the open sliding doors and onto the porch. She crossed it and stood in the middle of the lawn.

Arnia had followed her to the doors. Like a puff of smoke, the queen disappeared before her eyes. "And poof... She's gone," she said while walking back to her chair.

"They've got some kind of transport ability," Shep stated. "But strange, they sent us back down in a small pod."

"Maybe it only works for them?" Frank suggested.

"Mm, possibly. Or have we been talking with another projection?" Arnia wondered.

"I shook her hand," Phil said.

"Eh...nope. You didn't. She never touched you," Frank

said.

Phil frowned. "Come to think of it, no, she didn't. Could she have been a hologram?"

"Well, whatever she was, if she comes back with a positive answer, we need to begin getting a plan in place," Phil decided. "Arnia, Shep, I would like you two to be in charge of a lot of it. How about you quit your jobs and apply to immigrate to the USA? I will give you a letter stating that we've hired you to work for the institute as security guards. Once the town has been built, you will be head of security for it. Basically, you'll still be police...just private police. You don't have to worry about money. I don't boast about it, but I'm quite wealthy. I'll look after the two of you. What do you think?"

"Can we think about it?" Shep asked. "Arnia and I need to talk. It's a huge decision. And you make it all sound so simple, but I doubt it will be that easy. There are too many illegal immigrants in both Canada and the USA. They don't accept legitimate immigrants easily now."

Phil smiled. "I've got some contacts, some pull in several places. Don't worry about that part of it. Just let me know once you complete the paperwork. Or...computer application nowadays. Talk it over. We need to wait for the queen's answer anyway."

"Let's go for a walk," Shep suggested to Arnia.

She joined him, and they went outside, crossed the lawn, and headed into the forest where there was a walking trail.

They had already walked it many times since staying at the institute, but now...they needed it for privacy and to give this new development a place in their minds without the urging of Phil and Frank. Phil's enthusiasm was somewhat overwhelming and almost contagious. She needed to make her decision without it, decide with Shep...

After they had walked for a while, Arnia stopped and

turned to face Shep. "Well, here we are. Have you thought about it while we walked?"

He placed his hands on her shoulders and looked into her eyes. "I have. It's very tempting. I like being a cop, but I don't like the living conditions in the city. And not even in the suburbs. My room in Langley was a bit better, but not by much. I want to be with you, always, but I don't see a future for us in Vancouver and its surroundings. We'd be lucky to find a bigger room somewhere, but still be living in mostly squalor. What are your thoughts? What do you think of Phil's plan and the project?"

"In my mind, it seems an insurmountable project. Can he really pull it off? He sounds positive, but what if the authorities start getting wind of it and interfere? What if we wind up behind bars instead of living in a little paradise?"

"Wow, you're really looking at the dark side of it."

"What about what you mentioned earlier? Applying for a transfer to a small town somewhere in BC?"

"I didn't want to tell you, but those opportunities seldom open up and, if they do, are given to someone from that town. I already looked into it when I was in Langley." He took her into his arms. "I love you, my little lamb."

Arnia wrapped her arms around his waist and snuggled against his strong chest. She listened to his steady heartbeat and thought about her little room in Vancouver, how depressed she'd been over the last few days at having to go back to it, to the pollution, the squalor. This was really an opportunity to get away from all that...to live in beautiful countryside, breathe fresh air every day, and they would be together...

And have a purpose...

To help people in need...

Because, yes, the Chekondo needed their help, or they would perish.

She looked up at him. "But, Shep, what if it fails? Then we're out of a job."

"We can always go live in the hollow tree," he said and chuckled. "Remember, there's one tree that pretty much has our names on it."

"What do you think? Have you decided?" she asked.

"I really want to do this. But only if you decide to as well."

"Yes. In a way, I think of the Chekondo as our people, too. We are partially Chekondo." Her heart sped up as she made the decision. "Yes, let's do it."

He tilted her chin and claimed her lips. Tenderly at first, and while kissing her, he lowered her to the side of the trail onto the mossy ground, then leaned over her and kissed her again. "I've so longed for you," he said huskily.

"I've been aching for you, too..." she admitted, barely above a whisper.

He groaned softly in response as his kisses became deeper and needier. His hands roamed beneath her shirt, tracing every curve of her body. She shivered, not from the cold, but from the anticipation of more.

She tugged at his clothes impatiently. Her eyes drank in the sight of him, the way his muscles strained with need for her. She ran her hands down his torso till she reached his shorts, pulling them off to reveal his hard arousal.

"I missed you," she confessed, meaning more than just the physical need.

He kissed her again, slower this time. Then he moved lower, kissing downwards until he was tasting every inch of her body. Each kiss echoed a promise and a sense of worship.

They undressed each other, their clothes quickly discarded among the trees as skin met skin in a fiery exchange. Their bodies moved together in remembered rhythm, under the forest canopy—no urgency, just love reborn where past melded into present became something eternal.

"It's cooling off. We should get back," Arnia said after a while. Reluctantly, she moved out of his arms and began to sit, but he pulled her back.

"Before we go back, there's another proposal I want to put before the two guys."

"And that is?"

"That they find a Justice of the Peace or a preacher or someone who can marry us before we return to Vancouver and begin making all the arrangements to make the big move to Oregon. I'll be damned if I want to spend another night alone in bed."

"Shepherd Daniels, is that a proposal?"

*

The next morning, just after breakfast, Zenthia knocked on the sliding doors.

Phil hurried to open them. "Good morning, Zenthia. We have just finished breakfast. Would you like coffee?"

"I do not know what that is."

"Tea maybe? Please, take a chair. Have you made a decision?" Frank asked while filling a cup with tea and handing it to the queen.

"Yes, my council members and I talked a long time and then informed our people of the plan. Like you, they brought many obstacles to my attention. But they are obstacles we can overcome through time and cooperation. The vote is yes. We will gladly accept your help and would like to settle here on Earth."

"Tell me, Zenthia, are you real or are you a projection, a hologram?" Phil asked. "We wondered because when I went to shake your hand yesterday, you avoided physical touch.

"I am real. That was our customary greeting. Is it different here?"

"Yes, it is."

"All the Chekondo have been awakened now that we are all healed. The only time we would appear as a projection is if we were still in stasis. The two projections Shep and Arnia met previously will now assist with various functions. They were programmed to perform many duties. Their databases have already recorded everything there is to know about this world. To begin, I have ordered them to begin teaching my people about Earth and all its customs."

"You will need to keep your little servitors hidden until you can slowly introduce one of them as an invention and then produce the others," Arnia said.

"You're jumping the gun, Arnia," Phil told her. "It'll take a few months to get everything ready to begin clearing the land and build a hangar for the ship. I'll start applying for permits right away."

"Don't forget the most important permit," Shep reminded him.

Phil gave him a blank look for a moment. "Oh, right… The license and a JP to get you hitched. We'll do that first thing this morning."

EPILOGUE

Three years later...

Arnia climbed the last leg of the hike to the summit of the mountain. When she reached the top, she let out a long breath and looked down at Chekondo.

The name choice had been unanimously accepted. Zenthia had voiced that she'd really like to somehow keep the name because it was part of their heritage. Shep had come up with Chekondo as the town's name. Phil had researched, and there was no town or village on Earth with the name, and he had registered it.

A little bit of Chekondo, right here on Earth...

And in a way, it was.

The town looked small from so high up. Miniature almost. But she could still make out the extremely futuristic design of some of the more elaborate structures—like the temple and the queen's residence.

It was finished...

Almost...

It would never be completely done as the small population grew, because they would need to build more homes.

It had been a very busy and complex few years. Teaching a hundred twenty-six aliens all the ways of Earth had been quite a task, and they were still learning.

And so were Frank and Phil...

Two of the Chekondo were scientists, and Frank and Phil had happily employed them in the institute with the caution to introduce new technology and possible new discoveries very slowly so not to awaken suspicion…

Would it always remain a secret?

There weren't many children among the survivors, about fifteen. Would they know never to talk? Some of them were too small. They probably wouldn't remember anything as they grew…

And then there was the problem of the Chekondo's extraordinary extra abilities, including their ability to run faster than any human ever could, jump higher, their laser eyes, strength, and other supernatural traits. Phil and Frank had impressed upon them never to use or reveal their abilities.

And Arnia knew from experience how hard that was… But she and Shep had finally revealed their own powers to the two scientists.

Maybe one day, far into the future, the people on Earth would be ready for the truth…

"There you are." Shep came climbing up the trail, carrying a cooler. "You're here early. I brought lunch."

"I'm not really hungry."

"How long have you been here?"

"Not that long. I've just been sitting here thinking about the last couple of years. It's the best decision we've ever made. Look at the beauty that surrounds us."

He set the cooler down and took her into his arms. "It's been an eventful three years. You look a bit pale. Are you okay?"

"I'm fine. Are you excited to finally move into our own place?"

He grinned down at her. "Sure am. It's hard to imagine that we'll have an actual house."

"Yes, with four bedrooms. It makes me want to fetch some of the homeless kids and bring them here. We'll be living here in luxury while there are so many without a roof over their heads, suffering, hungry."

"Honey, that'd be great, but we can't do that. You know how dangerous it would be. And you know what Zenthia predicted — Earth will heal."

"I still don't know how she can predict that. But it probably won't happen in our lifetime."

"Have you also forgotten that we have a much longer lifespan thanks to being hybrids?"

"Right. I still can't imagine that we're also Chekondo. To this day, I sometimes pinch myself to ensure I'm awake."

"Well, Mrs. Daniels, you're wide awake."

She snuggled closer to his chest. "And we're going to be seeing another little hybrid soon."

He held her away and, frowning, looked into her eyes. "Frank and Phil haven't started to — "

"No! They have sworn to never ever mess with embryos again." She took his hand and placed it on her belly. "This little hybrid."

"You're...we are...you're pregnant?"

"I believe so."

He hollered so loud she was sure they could have heard down in the town. "A baby? Our baby?"

"Eh...yes, whose would it be growing in my stomach?"

He grinned from ear to ear. "Another little half Chekondo. Wow. How far along are you?"

"I think about three or four months. I've never been regular, so I didn't take any notice. I take it you're happy."

"Little lamb...another lamb to add to my flock. You couldn't have given me better news!"

ABOUT THE AUTHOR

Gabriella Bradley lives amidst rugged mountains. She more than often has a grizzly in her yard searching for food and breaking into her garbage tote. Other critters that visit on a regular basis are cougars, coyotes, squirrels, raccoons.

Gabby's hobbies include graphic art, gardening, swimming, sewing, embroidery, and knitting. Her favorite movies are old-timers like Gone with the Wind and Spartacus. She is an avid Trekkie and loves series like Lost, Fringe, The 12 Monkeys, and Shadowhunters. Her favorite music is Abba.

www.ingramcontent.com/pod-product-compliance
Lightning Source LLC
Chambersburg PA
CBHW072102170626
46813CB00004B/1431